MY NAME IS LUKE

# MY NAME IS
# LUKE

{ A NOVEL BY }
## JIM RUDDLE

First Edition   ISBN 13: 978-1-937484-20-0
AMIKA PRESS   466 Central AVE #23 Northfield IL 60093   847 920 8084
info@amikapress.com   Available for purchase on amikapress.com
Edited by John Manos. Cover illustration by Nathan Matteson. Cover photographs by Tamara Herrera. Author photograph by Pedro Garcia. Designed and typeset by Sarah Koz. Body in Joanna MT, designed by Eric Gill in 1930, digitized by Monotype Typography in 1991. Titles in Lapis, designed by Jim Rimmer in 2006. Thanks to Nathan Matteson.

To the many who have offered words,
charts, ropes, songs, and advice.
Perhaps you were never thanked—now you are.

MY NAME IS LUKE.

I guess that's the way I should start this off. A fellow here in Massachusetts wrote a book about a white whale, and he began it with "Call me Ishmael." I read most of it, but it was too windy for me. I'd put him about a nine on the Beaufort Scale. He blew so hard he could have pushed a fleet of clippers around the Horn. Besides, the old guys around the docks tell lots better stories, and they don't babble on for hours the way that Ishmael does. Some people say the book wasn't really about blubber hunting, anyway. It was full of ambiguities, they said, full of deeper things. What I think it was full of is whale manure, and I guess that goes about as deep as you can get. If you write about a crazy man with an ivory peg leg chasing across the Pacific for a pissed-off whale, I don't think you've got room for a lot of claptrap about everything else. Still, saying who you are seems to be a fair way to get going on one of these things, but don't expect that I'm going to tell you anything about whales, except that around here we don't think much of whaling. My Grandpa says—and he should know because he's sailed all over the world—that nothing on land is as stinking and ugly as a whale ship with its trying kettle smoking out in the middle of a blue ocean. And the whalemen! My God! They come back covered with greasy soot, their skins permanently saturated with rancid fat, and their clothes ready to be burned. Pigs would cross the road.

Of course, we do use the oil.

What I'm going to tell you about is what happened last summer, only it wasn't really what they say it was. I told them that at that investigation back home, but it didn't seem to make any difference. An old guy with a nose as red as the port light on a packet steamer, some kind of a government lawyer, tried to get me to say things I didn't believe. He wore steel-rimmed glasses that caught the light as he pushed his face right into mine and breathed peppermint at me, the sort that some of the men favor after they've tossed down a drink or two. He had a lot of white hair that needed to be trimmed at the corners. I didn't take to him from the moment I saw him, so I just sheeted in and waited for the blow to start.

"Now, young man, tell me how they kidnapped you."

"Well, they didn't."

"They didn't what?"

"They didn't kidnap me."

"You were taken off on that boat and nearly killed, and you weren't kidnapped?"

"No, sir."

"Why, that's rather hard to believe."

I'd be willing to bet that he'd heard and believed a lot more ridiculous things than that, and I'd even go further and wager that he'd said a few himself, but I was nervous and a little bit scared of being up there in that chair in front of a room full of unfamiliar people, and so I kind of squirmed down in my seat and gave him a straight look. He had a flinty gaze of his own.

"I'm just trying to tell the truth, sir."

"Do you deny that you were on the boat and that they wouldn't let you leave? If you don't know that's kidnapping, you don't know much about the law."

"Well, sir, if you think they could have put me ashore, you don't know much about nor'easters."

"That's hairsplitting, boy."

"I just wanted to make sure people understood."

"I think we'll excuse you for now and deal with this later."

He snorted and blew his nose on a big blue handkerchief, then waved me away from the stand.

And they never dealt with it later.

I wasn't trying to split any hairs. All I was saying was that the law can get awfully high-and-mighty when it describes something because there might be some shadows that don't show up. A man who makes an honest mistake can be turned into a hardened criminal by a law book and a lawyer. Of course, it works the other way too, and some of the country's biggest thieves and even murderers are sitting down to roast beef and beer because the same sort of law book says they are as innocent as babies. I know we have to have laws, but I've looked at the Constitution and it doesn't say anywhere that we have to have lawyers.

I don't really know that much about the law, so I'll just shut up about it for now.

And I see now that like that fellow who wrote about the white whale, if I want to tell my story I'm going to have to include a lot of things that you probably think are unexciting, and they are, but if you don't know who I am, why would you want to know the story? So what I'm trying to do is show you who I am.

Anyway, this all began the day I had been down on my Grandpa's boat, the *Mary Constance*, doing the job Grandpa Mike had given me. I'd stowed the coils of rope, small stuff for reefing or mousing, in the forepeak locker and secured the locker door so that the boxes holding paint pots, brushes, seldom-used fittings, sponges, and a jumble of other items would stay put when the boat pitched against a heading sea or rolled in a trough. A big roll of canvas took up a lot of room and weighed as much as a small locomotive, but there were other bits of sailcloth, large manila rope, and some heavy-duty blocks—some with sheaves and some just the cheeks—along with wooden wedges, canvas straps, and God knows what all. Actually, I knew what all because Mike had me label everything. I also jammed in two large jugs, one of turpentine, the other of linseed oil. Mike—I only call him "Mike" when he's not around—gets pretty cranky about keeping things where they're supposed to be, and for as long as I can remember he has drummed into my head that when a sailor needs something, in a storm, in the dark, he damned well doesn't want to have to search all over the boat to find it. He should be able to go to where it's supposed to be and lay a hand on it.

It was like working bent double in a cave. It wasn't hot, so I hadn't even bothered to raise the skylight because I hadn't thought the job would take very long when I started it. That's the hell of a boat: everything takes longer than you think it will. Also, as it turned out, I learned once more that you never know what will happen when you do something or what will happen when you don't. It sure makes life pretty unpredictable.

Laziness is another thing Mike can't abide, not that I'm a layabout who loafs on the job. Maybe he simply believes that if he keeps saying over and over that he can't stand sloth, I'll step lively to every task that he throws at me. And I usually do. Sometimes, I even start doing things before I know what I'm supposed to do.

But this was August, late in the afternoon of a surprisingly cool but sunny day, and school didn't start for weeks. The guys I usually hung around with were all either out on fishing boats or locked up with shore jobs of some kind or just doing chores around their homes. Most times, especially when Mike was around, I went to the chandlery to try to help out. I know where most of the things are in the shop, even things that are kept in boxes right up near the ceiling. I wrap things in paper and deliver them to places on shore. When Grandma Ellen fills in at the shop, I get to do all the ladder climbing, but when Grandpa Mike is there and running things, he usually scampers up the ladder without asking for help. He likes to think he's as spry as I am.

I guess I'm about average size for my age and, because I've done all kinds of jobs since I was small, I'm fairly strong. At least, I've done all right in arm wrestling, running, and things like that. Working on boats has been the best exercise in most ways, although many people seem to think that all sailors do is hang on the rail and tell lies except when they're ashore swilling something that makes their eyes roll up. Of course, I don't do that, but I do the other things sailors really do, and that is lift heavy boxes, haul away on lines that raise big sails, and climb up high in the rigging when something needs to be done up there. I haven't got to the point where I can grab the leech of a sail and, just using my grip, slide all the way down to the deck. That's a pretty impressive performance, and I don't recommend it unless your fingers are strong enough to pick up a fifty-pound keg of nails by the rims and you've got calluses on your fingertips as tough as a schooner captain's tongue. I'm not there yet.

I've only been out on the Banks a couple of times, and those have set off some caterwauling at home by Grandma Ellen—wails that I'm too young to be out there with those rough men and complaints that there should be laws that keep youngsters off boats and ships until they're old enough to have long whiskers. Considering all that's gone on in my background, I guess you could excuse some of her concerns, although I just have to look at things from my own point of view and not worry too much about what other people think. I don't want to worry anybody, but I don't want them worrying me, either.

That August day the harbor was quiet, the way it usually is when the fishing fleet is out on the Banks during the summer going after cod, not that there's much of a fleet these days. Old-timers talk about the time, not so long ago, when about a hundred schooners worked out of Marblehead, but nowadays there are maybe twenty-five or so. With even that small-er number of codbangers, if they had been in port there'd have been some yelling back and forth, some thumping and bumping of boats and barrels. The fact that the fleet was smaller was also a reminder that the number of fishermen had been reduced as well. I guess having to earn a living can be rough in lots of places, but it doesn't seem very forgiv-ing on the face of the sea.

The way it was that day, about the only thing disturbing the peace was an occasional dog bark, and down where I was those were barely audible. You might say that it was pretty dull.

We had some excitement that summer, though. Some fellows laid a wire cable across the bottom of the Atlantic Ocean from Newfoundland to Ireland! No kidding. They've already got one from England to France, and so far it seems to work, at least they're not trying to cut each other's throats the way they've been doing for centuries.

Well, with this new one, the English Queen sent a tele-graph message to our President, and he sent one right back at her. Imagine. It only took about a day for the two mes-sages to be sent and received.

From what we heard, the cable is made of copper-wire rope and covered with gutta percha. Where the hell do they come up with these names? It's sort of like India rubber, and they get it from trees way on the other side of the world. It's kind of funny. It gets soft when it's heated and then, like in the cold water of the North Atlantic, it turns hard but not brittle. And, best of all, it keeps the water from messing up the telegraph. At least that's what they said when they built it. And they wrapped the whole lot in galvanized wire. Unfortunately, the signals whimpered out after a few weeks, and nobody's sure what to do now to solve the problem.

It's all about electricity, and I don't understand electricity. I don't think anybody understands electricity, even though they can make it do things.

Hell, you could say the same thing about having a dog fetch a ball. You can get him to do it, but you'll never know why he does.

I've been wondering whether it would be possible to send sounds over a cable. Wouldn't that be the damnedest! Just think about it. Instead of those clicks and clacks on a telegraph, you'd be able to actually hear somebody far away talk to you. Like the Queen of England! What would she sound like? She speaks English, so you should be able to understand her, although one day in town I heard a man from way down in the Carolinas talk, and I could barely understand a word. He said it was English.

And I wonder whether the cable down deep in the ocean could pick up underwater sounds, the bubbling, gurgling and splashing. Because nobody's ever spent any time at the bottom of the sea, we get all the crazy ideas people can make up. Maybe oysters are performing a chorus of "What Shall We Do with a Drunken Sailor," or mermaids are singing harmony, or those crazy sirens that caused the Greeks to run ships onto the rocks are tuning up for the next Odysseus to come blundering along. I tell you, there's a lot we've got to learn.

I read in the newspaper that cable just like the one they used for the telegraph had been cut up into little pieces and is being sold by jewelry stores in New York. So help me. Some of the pieces are even set into gold geegaws with pins on them so that ladies can wear them around town apparently showing how advanced they are. And bigger chunks of the cable have been peddled to businessmen to use as paperweights. Sometimes, it's hard to figure out what things are really valuable and what things are junk.

Take all those guys who went to California with the gold fever a few years ago. They endured rounding the Horn or going through the Central American jungles or bumping across the continent in jolting, dusty wagons just so they could—maybe—find a few grains of gold. In the process they ignored millions of acres of dirt that lay between New England and California. You can grow things in dirt: corn, potatoes, beans, and so on. You can graze cattle on grass that grows in dirt. But as far as I can tell, the only thing you can do with gold is look at it and say it's pretty or that you're going to call it money. But gold is supposed to be valuable, and dirt is supposed to be cheap.

The men at the harbor have been talking about the telegraph cable and how it beat everything in history in getting messages from one side of the ocean to the other. One of them, Hancey Darnell, got all excited over the thing. Why, according to him, it was the greatest invention of all mankind, and it was a triumph of Western Civilization, and it was finally going to end the scourge of war.

"How's that?" Mike asked.

"Because people will be able to discuss things with each other. Countries like the United States and England or France or Germany or anybody else over there won't be getting into fights with people on the other side of the ocean because they'll be able to communicate their problems immediately and head off matters before they heat up. I'm telling you, it's the beginning of the Age of Peace."

Grandpa looked at me and asked: "Luke, do you think this cable is going to do what Hancey says? That people will talk with each other and not go to war?"

"Well, sir," I said. "I can see that it might help, but those three fellows on the other side of the hill who got put in jail last week for trying to knock each other over the head had been talking all evening before they started going at each other. As a matter of fact, if they hadn't been gassing the way they were, they probably wouldn't have fought at all.

"Besides, we've got telegraph wires strung all over this country, and we still have people in the North not getting along with people in the South and people in the South who think Northerners are all idiots. You could work that telegraph until the wires started to smoke, and it wouldn't make folks love each other. At least, that's how it seems to me."

Mike nodded, Hancey started getting scarlet in the face, and I decided that I had some chores to do and got the hell out of there.

Wire cables, and not just copper ones, are getting a lot of attention around here, even without all the babble about the telegraph. I guess they've been working with them to hold up bridges and things like that. One fellow built a bridge over the Niagara River with wire cables bracing it up, but not many have been put on sailboats, yet. The British navy has been using them some, and a lot of the steamships have them—big, thick twisted wire. Grandpa Mike, who's generally ahead of things, has made all of the standing rigging on the *Mary Constance* out of smaller galvanized wire, and, even though it pained him, he replaced the lanyards and dead-eyes on the shrouds with turnbuckles and wire rope. He says they're the way to go, even though they don't look as shipshape. That didn't seem to bother him for the rest of the boat, and he put turnbuckles on the remainder of the rigging without a mumble.

Turnbuckles—the limeys call them "bottlescrews"—are hollow tubes with a screw thread at each end, and each screw is cut in a different direction. Rings at each end are used to attach the ends of the stays or shrouds to a chainplate, and the fact that the turnbuckle's screws work in opposite directions means you can either tighten or loosen the stress on the cable depending on which way you twist the turnbuckle.

Able Hampton, one of Grandpa's friends, says if you rig a boat with metal cable, it's going to rust in the salt air—everything made out of metal does, except bronze and lead, and copper turns green. Gold doesn't rust, but I've already said that it's worthless for any useful purpose. Of course, you've got that telegraph cable, which also uses galvanized wire along with the gutta percha and the copper, and if it can stand up to the bottom of the ocean, it should be able to hold up a couple of masts for a while.

The ropes most boats use now for the shrouds are covered with blacking that's a smelly mess made of thin tar, whiskey—so help me—hot salt water, lamp black, and a kind of powder that comes from lead. I call it lead dust, although that's more than likely wrong. You have to wonder how all that got mixed together in the first place. Probably some old navy captain started pouring tar and hot salt water together, took a swig from a bottle of whiskey, and decided that if it kept him going it might work on the rigging. And, because he thought black standing rigging looked pretty racy, he tossed in some lampblack. Why he added the lead dust? More than likely, he had some handy and didn't know what the hell else to do with it.

When Mike decided to tar the wire cables, he really got picky about how we put it on, and I was doing most of it. I had to spread old cloths all over the deck, and if I got a drop of anything on it or on one of the spars, he made more noise than a dog at a rat hole. We put most of it on before we attached it to the spars, but the end fittings had to be treated again after they were fastened. Another reason he switched from hemp to wire was probably because he figured that he could change the formula for blacking the cables because he hated to waste any whiskey by pouring it into a mess of tar and lampblack. He says whiskey and wire don't mix. Not that he's a real drinker like a lot of these soaks who work on boats, but he does like a little nip from time to time, although I can't say why. I sneaked a drink from one of his bottles once, and it just about killed me. I expected to see smoke and fire come out of my mouth and my guts explode. How grown men can say they like it is beyond me. And the ones who drink a lot of it wobble around like the ass end of a spavined horse and generally make fools of themselves. You see a lot of that with fishermen.

I guess sailors and strong drink go a long way back. If you believe Genesis, you know that there was a hellacious flood once upon a time. Old Noah was the first mariner I know about who got into shipping livestock, and the insides of that ark would have driven Grandpa nuts. A little coal dust is enough to send him into a conniption fit. Can you imagine every animal in creation eating and unloading in that barge? The smell would have been significant. And afterward Noah plants a vineyard, makes wine, gets half-seas over, and is discovered by his sons, who are embarrassed, while he is just bare-assed, lying drunk in his tent. That seems perfectly understandable after a voyage with elephants, lizards, mice, alligators, and monkeys. And that's just for starters. You don't hear much about that in Sunday school.

And many Yankee sailors first went before the mast on ships carrying slaves to the Caribbean to trade for molasses with which to make rum—or for rum itself. You can bet that they sampled the wares. Mike told me that when he was a boy, rum was about the only thing that was consumed around most harbors in the Northeast. Some of the richest families in New England got their fortunes that way. When we cut off the import of slaves, farmers out west found that it was easier to ship whiskey to market than wagonloads of corn and wheat. Stills were steaming all over America, so the boys in the fo'c'sle didn't miss a beat, filled their gourds with cheap liquor, and downed that just as heartily.

Mr. Hampton wouldn't let up on the idea that wire cable was a bad choice for a sailboat rig. He and Mike and some other men were sitting around on some scrap lumber, and he started in on Mike's ideas.

"The first thing," he said, "it's going to start rusting as soon as it's made. You won't be able to see it, but as soon as the air hits it, if it has any moisture at all, it'll start to corrode. It'll still be rusting inside, and you won't have any idea of what's happening. You'll be running with a stiff breeze, admiring your strong wire cable, and—*Bam!*—the whole damned rig, spars and all, will come crashing onto the deck. If you're lucky, it won't knock your brains out or punch a hole in your hull."

He paused and looked around at the others.

"It's a good idea to think about," he said, "but it needs a little more work."

Mike leaned back and smiled.

"Well," he said, "I could say the same thing about tarred rope: it's supposed to last longer than plain rope because the tar keeps it from rotting, but sooner or later it will, and because of the tar and blacking you won't be able to see that it's rotten until it breaks."

You could tell that Able didn't care for that kind of analysis.

"Horseshit," he said, showing off his debating skills.

# { CHAPTER 2 }

I WAS SORT OF THINKING OF THESE THINGS THAT DAY DOWN in the boat and wondering whether Grandpa Mike was really smart or just a lucky chance-taker. He was smart enough to make a go of the chandlery and the delivery business, so that shows something. Of course, you have to throw in the fact that he works hard, too. And there are different kinds of smart, as well. For instance, there's a fellow in Marblehead who can add numbers in his head faster than you can figure them on a slate, and I'm talking lots of numbers, like columns of five or six across. He can do that, but in other matters he's just not in it. He thinks turnips grow on the moon. So, what's smart?

A rolled-up storm sail lay against the frames of the compartment on a long low shelf just forward of the butt of the foremast that came down through the deck and was stepped below me on the keel. It didn't make for the best bed in the world, but it was a fairly soft place to lie for a few minutes, a lot softer than the small kedge anchor and three hundred feet of rode that were secured against the stringers on the other side.

I was just killing time, thinking about things. Most people don't consider what goes on in kids' heads as "thinking." But we think all the time, not about grown-up problems like politics or tariffs or stuff like that, but about who we are and what we want to do—things we'd like to do even if it's not likely that we'll do them. Sometimes, we think about the past, although we don't have a lot of it. Even so, we've got the same kinds of memories that other people have. We just don't have as many, maybe. We think ahead about adventures and being fishermen or sea captains and going to far parts of the world, of learning to speak other languages and wearing different clothes and doing well in school. We think about things we've read and heard about, of grizzly bears, coconuts, and cotton bales. We've seen things come in on ships, and we want to know about where they came from, and we've known about heroes and Indians and clipper ships and Old Ironsides and how the gunners at Fort Sewell, right here in Marblehead, kept the British from getting at her.

Sure, we think.

And we spend some time thinking about who we want to be. Me? I guess I do a lot of daydreaming. Mike calls it woolgathering. I can't very well talk about it much except to somebody like my friend Ez.

I guess if I were to pick the person I'd most like to be, it would be Captain Creesy. He was skipper of the Flying Cloud when it broke all the records going to San Francisco, around the Horn, in eighty-nine days and eight hours. We all know exactly how long it took. Some other guy claimed that he did it faster, but he said it was departure-to-landfall that should be counted, not anchor-to-anchor, which is a lot of riprap, because you can make a landfall, be close enough to a harbor to count the freckles on a fellow standing on shore, then sit outside for hours or days waiting for tide and wind to let you in. You raised the land, all right, but you haven't completed the voyage until the hook is in the bottom or you're alongside a dock. The whole idea of a fast passage is so that the cargo or the people you're carrying get where they're going in a hurry. That's what you get paid for. Until you can start unloading, you haven't finished the job.

Anyway, Captain Creesy is the man. Nobody else has been able to drive a clipper the way he did with the Cloud, and nobody else ever will. At least, I don't think so.

You know, of course, that Captain Creesy was born in Marblehead. That his wife went with him on the record-breaker, and that she was the navigator. That's right. He was the captain, but she used the sextant and told them where they were.

When the Flying Cloud broke the record, all the newspapers had the story and damned if some of them didn't get the Captain's name wrong. So help me! The first one wrote about "Captain Cressy," and some others followed with the same error. It got so bad that one reporter from Boston came out to Salem to see the Captain—he had moved there, though God knows why anybody would—and left saying the Captain was stupid because he didn't even know how to spell his own name. Is that gall, or not?

It didn't bother the Captain. He keeps on pronouncing and signing his name "Creesy" the way he has all his life, and the newspapers kept on printing nonsense, and I'll bet that if you run across his name, somebody will have spelled it "Cressy." And to make matters worse, there are people whose name is really "Cressy" living around New England, and they might even be related.

It reminded me of the old story about Captain Ireson. Last year, a guy named Whittier made up a poem about him and said that he had refused to help the members of a sinking ship and that Marblehead women tarred him and feathered him because he had let other sailors die. Everybody in town knows the real story of how Captain Ireson wanted to go to the ship's assistance but that the crew of his ship, Betsy, in what amounted to a mutiny, forced him to wear away and leave the stricken sailors to the fury of the waves.

The women of Marblehead hadn't waited to find out what really happened, started egging each other on, and did something they wouldn't have done by themselves. But the real problem was that they took something that wasn't true and spread that around. By the time this Whittier got around to writing about it, he went with what ignorant people already believed. He said he had learned about the incident from somebody when he was a kid in school. For God's sake.

{ CHAPTER }
{ 3 }

THE KIDS AT MY SCHOOL HAVEN'T GIVEN ME ANY STORIES like that. Of course, they probably know more about what goes on at sea than that Whittier fellow does.

My friend, Ez—that's short for Ezra—is off right now with his father on the *Katie Sorrel*, one of the luckiest boats in the fleet. Other boats come in off the banks with half-empty holds, but the *Katie* always fills up to the gunwales, it seems. It's like any other kind of fishing, I guess. You can sit right beside some guy on a creek bank, both of you using the same bait and fishing poles, and you won't catch so much as a shad while he just hauls them in. You always wonder why. Is it something about you, or are the fish saying something? But since I don't like fishing with a pole, anyway, I really don't worry about it.

I sure do miss old Ez. He's a little taller than I am, but he probably doesn't weigh any more. He's the most fun of any of the guys I know, and that's why we run around a lot together. It sometimes surprises me that we almost never get into trouble. He has a black mutt with a woolly coat and floppy ears and is a real case. Its name is Bugle. Ez heard some-where about a dog with that name that supposedly bayed with a sound that carried for miles and made him a cham-pion hunting dog. When Ez got Bugle as a pup, he glued that name onto him, although Bugle never lifted his muz-zle to bay at anything. The dog just yelps—what the French would call a cry de cur, I suppose. That is, he yelps if his teeth aren't sunk into a piece of wood.

Bugle has one major quirk: he likes sticks. Now, I know, nearly all dogs will chase a stick if you throw it for them, but Bugle will go after a stick that's just sitting there minding its own business. It doesn't have to move for Bugle to fix on it and charge. It makes it hard to walk with him in a straight line because there always seems to be some small stick or twig that attracts him—and off he goes. It's a wonder that Ez hasn't lost his voice from yelling, "Bugle! Drop that stick!" The good thing is that Bugle will drop it. Otherwise, he'd be trotting around looking like a brushpile, I suppose.

One day, Ez and I had been fooling around down by the causeway leading over to the Neck. Bugle was with us, and we had been tossing a stick into the water for him to retrieve, a game he would play until your arm dropped off. The har-bor was like glass that day, scarcely any breeze at all, and Bugle, unlike some water dogs, kept his muzzle way down low in the water as he swam. I don't think he was drinking sea water, but how would I know? Anyway, Ez had wound up and thrown the stick as far as he could, and that was a pretty good heave, I have to tell you.

Bugle took off with a flying splash and paddled all the way to the floating stick without veering so much as a degree from his course. When he got to the stick, Bugle snapped his jaws around it and headed back for shore, with his muzzle low, his eyes almost closed, and his head unmoving. When he swam that way, the stick stuck out on either side of his mouth, and while he wasn't exactly tossing up a bow wave, he did make a noticeable ripple in the water. Ez and I weren't paying a lot of attention because it was a pretty straightforward performance for Bugle. A scream brought us up short. The bellowing came from an old lady in a wide gray dress, a crocheted white cap on her head, who was perched on a rock along the roadway. She waved her hands heavenward, or I guess what she thought was that general direction. Her mouth was wide open, but she wasn't making any more sounds, other than a kind of huffing, and her gaze was firmly fixed on Bugle as he plowed his way back to shore.

"Save me, Lord! It's that snake ship!"

Ez looked at me, his eyes as wide and round as portholes.

"Did she say my dog is snakeshit?" he asked in disbelief.

"No, you idiot. She's talking about the monster. I'll tell you about it later. Let's just calm her down, for now."

Ez is always quick to pick up on a change in the situation, and he turned to the woman with a half-bow.

"Why, ma'am," says Ez, "that's my champion hunting dog, Bugle, whose baying can be heard for miles."

That Ez. I was grinning and chuckling as Bugle came heaving out of the harbor, shaking a rainbow of droplets around him as he gamboled up to us.

"Why, it's just a dog," the woman said. "I thought it was the sea monster. Maybe my eyes aren't as good as they should be."

"Yes, ma'am," we both agreed.

You may think the lady was a bit daft, but she wasn't the only one along this coast who had trouble with their eyes. Grandpa Mike says there have always been people willing to put their hands on Bibles or their hands in the fire to swear that they had seen a sea monster right here in Massachusetts Bay. There's an old man down in Nahant, named Buddin, who claims to have seen the serpent twenty times. I'm not sure whether he's supposed to have seen twenty different serpents or the same one twenty times, but he vows that he's seen it or them.

Gloucester was the worst spot for sightings, and normally you'd just say it was because the way they drink over there. They're liable to see most anything. But Mike says, and some of the other men who have been around here for a long time all agree, that for as long as anyone can remember even respectable people and ship captains have reported seeing some kind of sea serpents or sea monsters between Boston and Cape Ann.

And when the old lady said she thought she'd seen the "snake ship," she was just confused about what a Boston newspaper had done, being cute the way newspapers are. I guess there had been so many folks who claimed to have seen the monster, hundreds of them at the same time, that the newspapers began to take notice and send reporters who couldn't see anything and therefore made fun of those who said they did see it. One of the papers started calling the monster "His Snakeship" because so many people were paying attention to him.

That must have been what the woman was talking about because a swimming Bugle looks nothing like a ship. Or a snake, for that matter. And Ez was right in being puzzled, although he was wrong in what he heard.

When Grandpa Mike and the other men talked about the times the serpent was spotted along the coast, they all swore that they knew somebody who was honest and sober who claimed to have seen it.

That's what I told Ez. He just shook his head and took the stick away from Bugle.

As I said earlier, the sea has so many things we'll never know about, what with it being so big and so deep. I mean, who would believe a whale unless you had actually seen one? And then there are things in the ocean that look like they might be something else, like that clipper captain out in the middle of the ocean who reported sighting a serpent a hundred feet long, with a knobby head, all covered with fur. He was a sober man and a respected skipper, who even gave the exact time and position of the sighting.

Another ship in the same area at the same time saw what he had seen and lowered a longboat full of men to check out the monster. Apparently, they weren't too keen on the assignment, but they rowed up as close as they dared and then discovered that it was nothing but a big, empty barrel all covered with green, fuzzy sea growth that had picked up a long line of kelp that trailed behind it for several boat lengths. That's the kind of trick the sea plays on you.

# CHAPTER 4

THE INCIDENT WITH THE OLD LADY GAVE EZ AND ME AN idea, so I guess you could say what happened was her fault. Maybe we were just bored at the time—this was last spring—and so we decided to liven up the town. We figured that if Bugle, a pretty unremarkable looking dog, could be mistaken for His Snakeship, we could come up with something that would really cause a ruckus.

Bugle wasn't to have a leading part in this joke, at first. Ez left him tied to a tree in his yard, lying in the shade, eying the small branches that swayed above him, probably waiting for a chance to fly up and grab one.

It was simple, really. We scrounged around in back of a lumberyard and found a thick pine board about three feet long and two feet wide. Up at Grandpa's shop—he wasn't around—we used one of his saws to cut it into a kind of long triangle with some notches on the top edge. We drilled a couple of holes in the bottom side, ran some rope through them, and used the rope to tie a brick onto the bottom edge of the board which we then painted black with red spots, although nobody had ever reported seeing spots on a sea serpent. It sort of dressed it up. When we put it in the water, it did just what we wanted it to: it stood on edge, with the notched side pointing up and the red spots looking dangerous.

After that, it was easy to hook on a few hundred feet of old longline, no longer fit for fishing on the Banks, and to row a skiff out a short distance from Doliber Cove for our first effort. The cove is pretty deserted most of the time, but people pass along the shore on their way to and from Peaches Point. That's what we were counting on. We didn't want a big crowd for this initial trial, just someone, or a couple— that would be even better because they could support each other's stories—who could alert Marblehead to the threat of a new sea monster.

We placed lead sinkers on the line, just far enough apart to keep the line from breaking the surface, dropped the weighted and painted board over the stern, and rowed toward the Point. The "monster" was trailing far behind the skiff and performing well, its black and red fin protruding high above the surface. We both got excited when we saw a man strolling along, swinging a cane, and apparently free to observe our handiwork. He kept walking, kept swinging the cane, and didn't see a damned thing. People just naturally miss a lot of good things.

This happened a couple of more times and, although Ez and I switched rowing chores routinely, we were getting frustrated that nobody was paying any attention to the monster. We debated whether to call over to shore and ask, "What's that thing in the water?" but figured that we had to stay completely out of the picture unless we wanted suspicion to fall on us. While we were trying to decide what to do next, we heard a series of shouts on shore and saw that one of the wharfside loafers had wandered all the way to Doliber Cove and, maybe sober, more than likely drunk, had set up a commotion about a sea serpent.

That was the cue for Ez and me to each take an oar and pull like mad for the Point so we could round it and be out of sight if a crowd arrived. And, of course, the faster we rowed the more the board agitated the water, sort of wobbling from side to side, and the more it looked to be alive. As soon as we made the Point, we boated the oars and began hauling frantically, hand-over-hand, to pull the monster aboard and hide it under an old tarp. Everything worked the way we had planned it, and by the time we leisurely pulled back down the harbor all the action had moved to the wharf, where the man who had first sighted the monster was being treated to another cup of something fierce.

Ez and I sauntered around listening to the chatter. The guy we had heard yelling on the shore had apparently roused the notice of a few others, and by the time we had pulled the monster out of sight around the Point, everybody in the lower reaches of Marblehead had heard something of what he had seen. Sometimes I wonder why we need the telegraph with the speed people can pass things along without it. Anyway, the case had been made that the sea serpent, "His Snakeship," had returned, although Ez kept referring to him by the term he thought he had heard the old woman say. As a matter of fact, to this day whenever Ez hears something he doesn't believe, he says, "That's just snakeshit."

We got even more attention the second time we set out in

the skiff about a week later. On that day, a mother with two small children was parked under a tree, knitting, as far as we could make out from our view in the boat. We dumped the monster over the stern and pulled heartily past the old salt house at the town wharf, then we coasted along with the oars resting on the thwarts so as not to attract any attention to ourselves. This was a much trickier maneuver than the first one because, while the fishing fleet wasn't as big as it used to be, there were plenty of small boats and workboats bobbing around in the harbor. We didn't want our monster to get fouled on an anchor rode or a mooring line so we had plotted a straight course for our dreaded beast.

As the red and black fin wobbled its way past the midday crowd ashore, the woman with the kids yelled, "There it is!" and soon everybody seemed to be pointing and screeching. Ez put his oar over on the starboard side and gave a couple of strokes in order to turn the skiff behind a fairly large schooner that sat high in the water. As we had done the first time, Ez and I handed the longline as fast as we could, bringing the monster closer with every pull and inciting the shoreside crowd to greater enthusiasm because of its increased speed. The sun was shining right in their eyes, so that probably helped. We tried to ease the phantom serpent around the big outboard rudder on the schooner, but the line got hung up on something—a splinter, a barnacle, something—and I was only able to get it loose by using the end of my oar to push the line away from the rudder. As we did the first time, we heaved the painted board and its brick into the bottom of the boat and covered it.

Maybe it was the sunlight bouncing off the wet blade of

the oar, or maybe we were not as slick as we thought, but one of the men in the crowd sought us out after we beached the skiff farther down the harbor toward the causeway.

"You boys having some fun?" he asked.

His name was Edgar Sanders, a pinch-faced ninny who worked as a bookkeeper for one of the shoe companies, that is, when they were running. I think he's been working as a clerk for somebody since the factory closed, but he seems to have plenty of time to snoop around. His nickname is "Sneaky." He probably peeks through windows. Most people shy away from him because he isn't pleasant to be around and is known to tell tales all over town. You can't do that and be very popular.

Oh, there are those who cultivate gossips, hoping to hear something bad about somebody else, but even they have no respect for Sneaky, whose question still hung in the air.

"Yes, sir," I replied. "You don't get many better days than this to go out on the water."

"Fishing, I suppose?"

"Well, no, sir. We were just rowing around."

"You didn't happen to come across any sea monsters, did you?"

Ez and I exchanged looks that could have appeared guilty or just puzzled. Who knows how other people read our faces?

"Sea serpent? Haw, haw, haw," Ez responded.

It was a pretty game effort, but to my ear it sounded about as hollow as an empty quahog shell.

"Why," he went on, "we haven't seen anything but a bunch of old fishheads going out with the tide. And maybe a pine plank floating along."

He later told me he added that pine plank business so that he wouldn't actually be telling a lie. The monster was a pine plank, after all.

"Yes, well. It's funny that you didn't see anything when half the town over on shore did. They claim to have seen a sea serpent and all you saw was fishheads. I don't suppose you boys actually saw a monster and thought it was fishheads, did you?"

"No, sir, Mr. Sanders," Ez piped up. "I don't know a thing about sea serpents, but I know pretty much all I need to know about fishheads, and unless sea serpents are real close relatives to codfish I've never seen a one of them."

Mr. Sanders gave each of us a smirk and walked away.

# CHAPTER 5

"DO YOU THINK HE KNOWS?" EZ ASKED.

"How could he?"

"I don't like it," said Ez. "My Pa would scrape my hide with a scaling knife if he found that I've been playing tricks on the town."

"I agree," I said. "It's probably time to get out of it. What if that damned Sanders starts talking about us being out in the skiff? And if somebody remembers we were over by Doliber Cove when the first scare happened?"

We were right to be worried. I guess old Sneaky went straight from his meeting with us to one of the taverns and told anybody who would listen that he thought we were up to some kind of prank somehow involving the sea serpent, that we looked guilty, and that we were hiding something, maybe in the skiff. When Ez and I walked from the beach up Front Street, people gave us hard stares that gave us the fidgets, and it wasn't until we happened to see my friend Agatha with some of her girl friends that we learned that our activities were now the talk of Marblehead, although nobody could say just what we had done.

"I don't know what you're up to, Lucas, but you better be careful." She could call me Lucas anytime she wanted to.

Well, that did it. I wasn't going to take a fall in her eyes.

Ez and I raced back to the skiff, cut the brick loose from the serpent's belly, and bundled him up in the tarp. On the other side of the causeway, facing Nahant, the rocky beach gave us some shelter from curious eyes, and we built a driftwood fire as soon as we could and put that damned monster in the flames. So much for the evidence. It took a while to cook the board down to coals and then smash them into little pieces with rocks before we scattered them along the beach. We still faced the suspicions that we had rigged something to try to scare people, and it wouldn't be easy to get that out of their minds.

Ez and I sat on a rock and mulled the matter over in our heads for a few minutes. Inspiration invaded my brain.

"Bugle!" I cried.

"Where?" Ez asked, craning his neck and looking around. "Where's Bugle?" The mutt was supposed to be tied to the backyard tree.

"No. Bugle's not here, but we can use him to get out of this."

"How's that?"

So I explained it to him.

Two days later, when we had another mild day, with only puffs of wind and hardly any chop in the water, Ez and I set out to cover our watery tracks. We now had an accomplice: Bugle, the champion baying-hunting dog.

Ez stationed Bugle below the wharf down near the water and out of sight of the folks who gathered as they normally did up on top. Bugle may not really be a champion hunting dog, but he will stay put if you tell him to. I pushed the skiff into the water just down the harbor and Ez jumped in with me. His right hand was kept down below the gunwale so that it was out of sight. He was holding a stick. I rowed up toward the wharf to where Bugle stood immobilized on a rock. Everybody up above could see us but not the dog, and to make sure they noticed us, I waved and even hollered a "Hello!" as though I was recognizing a friend on shore.

A few heads turned in our direction, and that's when Ez, very casually, eased his right hand over the stern and waggled the stick. That's all Bugle needed. In a flash, he leaped into the harbor and began swimming as fast as he could in the wake of the skiff. Perhaps a hundred yards separated us as Bugle took up the chase, and I rested on my oars to give him a chance to close. '

"Come on, Bugle!" yelled Ez.

A few of the men wandered to the edge of the wharf to get a look.

What they saw was two boys in a boat, a gap of water, and then Bugle's black woolly head plowing through the water.

"Well, I'll be damned," said one of the men.

"I'll be double-damned," said another. "That's what that fool Sanders was talking about. He thought a couple of kids playing with a dog was some sort of a sea monster trick."

"He must be dumber than the dog."

"Where's Sanders? I don't see any red spots on that dog."

"Old Sneaky would probably pee a ring around hisself if he saw it."

There was some more of that sort of thing, and a lot of jeers and catcalls when we hoisted Bugle aboard so he could drench us with his patented shake. Ez and I turned and rowed on down the harbor, Bugle holding the stick in his mouth, and nobody gave us another look.

Later, sneaky Mr. Sanders sought us out and said he hadn't seen any dog around on the day he had talked to us.

"Of course, not," Ez answered. "He left the boat to go after a stick. I guess you missed that part."

"Well," said Sanders, as he saw Bugle dart across the road dragging a small branch in his mouth. "He does seem to be a dedicated dog."

"Yes, sir," I agreed. "He is."

"And," Ez added, "you should hear him bay. You can hear him in three counties. That's what makes him a champion hunting dog."

The funny thing is, a couple of weeks after we burned the make-believe serpent in the beach fire and used Bugle to put us in the clear, everything had calmed down when two highly respected citizens, two men of what they call "sterling" character, said they had seen a scaly serpent, at least fifty feet long writhing through the water near Gloucester. What did they see, if anything? Damned if I know. I don't think it was Bugle, though. They didn't report seeing any sticks.

# { CHAPTER 6 }

YOU'D THINK THAT I'D HAVE A DOG OF MY OWN TO KEEP ME company. Sure, I'd like to have a dog to toss a ball for or chase ducks or just mosey around the docks with. No dog, though. Grandpa Mike won't allow it.

"A dog would just as soon shit on the deck as on the dock," was his view on the subject, adding that until such time as he saw one that could go to the bow, take a line in its teeth, leap onto a dock, and make a round turn and two half-hitches around a bollard, he wasn't having any dogs on his boat. Otherwise, he likes dogs. He just likes them away from his boat. Besides, there's nobody home much of the time, and he says it doesn't seem fair to leave a dog all by himself all of the time. I know I wouldn't like it. At least, not all of the time.

But I bring up the subject every now and then, telling him that the dog wouldn't be alone, that Grandma Ellen would like some company when Mike and I are away from the house, and that the dog could even go with her to the chandlery and sleep in the back room. Sometimes, I think he's bending a little, but so far I haven't won him over.

One fellow, an old-timer who sailed a brightwork brag boat of some sort, had a rangy white dog on board all the time. He solved the problem of keeping the dog's mess off the decks by taking one of those coconut mats people have begun putting in front of their doors to wipe their feet on, working a grommet into one corner with an awl, and tying a small line in it. He trained the dog to crap on the mat, and when the dog was finished with his business the old man simply tossed the mat over the side, dragged it through the water for fifteen minutes or so and brought it up clean as new.

This worked pretty well, at first. The problems came when they went ashore and the dog found coconut mats sitting in front of a lot of doors and started using them as toilets. Great way to start a day: open the door and step in dog shit.

Normally, if I had an afternoon like this one to waste a few hours, I would have brought a book, propped myself up in the cockpit, and read until the light failed. *Robert Merry's Museum*, a magazine I've been reading for a couple of years, has just put out an entire book made up of the "Go-Ahead Gil" stories that had run in the magazine. That Gil, he's been everywhere and done everything, from riding elephants and camels to dodging bullets and outrunning Arab thieves. Not that you're supposed to believe all these tales are true, but that's the fun of a good adventure story: you know it's not true, but it might be, and more than that, in your own mind, you might be right in the middle of it.

Adventure sounds like fun, and I want to have some, but deserts aren't in it, for me, anyway. And why would I want to go look at fields of cotton in Arkansas, for instance? A fellow here said we had sent missionaries there, but the natives ate them. I don't really believe that. And there are men who went out West to catch beavers so their pelts could wind up on some fool's head as a hat. Others went after buffalo hides, those things as thick and heavy as a coil of one-inch rope—yet they try to peddle them as lap robes. You'd probably die under one.

If you were up in the Rocky Mountains sleeping in a snow bank that was ass-deep on a tall Indian, I suppose a buffalo robe might work, although I'd rather not head for those hills anyway. Who the hell wants to wrestle a bear for dinner? I want to go where there are bananas and oranges.

Today, knowing I had a job to do, I didn't bother bringing a book. I read a lot and am pretty good at it. I ought to be, seeing as how I spend so much time during the winter reading to the folks who sew shoes.

Marblehead, in case you don't know it, is one of the biggest shoemaking towns in the country, maybe even in the world, and hundreds of people make their living working for one or another of the companies that make the shoes. Other towns are doing shoes in a big way—North Reading, Lynn, and Randolph, just to name a few. After the Marblehead fleet got wrecked, people had to do something to make a living, and the shoe shops came in. Now, some guys have invented machines that not only sew cloth but can do some leather shoe parts, as well. I guess as long as they can't do the whole shoe with machines there'll be work for the people in the small shops. Machines are scary things that can either be good or bad for the workers. I just don't know yet.

Only the final stages of shoemaking are done in one big room. The rest takes place in little shops scattered all around, many of them sheds that are tacked onto the sides or backs of houses. Maybe eight or ten or even more people, mostly young women, but sometimes whole families, bend to the sewing of the uppers which get the soles put on later at the factory. The men are older, as apparently the idea of young men and young women being together in close quarters all day is reason for worry, although I don't see why. It would liven things up.

The workers come from all kinds of backgrounds—some used to have money and now don't, some came over from the old country and are just getting started, others say they just like the job and stick with it year after year. Some of them can't read at all, but there are others who are pretty well educated. The problem is, they can't read, cut, and sew at the same time, so in the winter I often spend a couple of hours reading to them—newspapers and books. The newspapers are so small and have so little in them that I don't have to waste a lot of time reading about local happenings, what Selectman So-and-So says we ought to do about the poor farm or what the fire chief says about the new engine pump or what some official in Essex County proposes for road building. Besides, when you get people listening to what the politicians are up to, some of them get mad and others think everything is dandy. Then they start cussing at each other, don't get their work done, and I can't read over the squabble.

Maybe you've figured out that Marblehead has a pretty mixed bunch of citizens, although most were born here and trace their roots back to Europe—England mostly. The number of fishermen grew, but not so much, and they've come here from all over. We have a handful of Portugee, not as many as Gloucester, and a couple of Spaniards, some from those islands called the A-zores, a few black people, three or four Indians, and a huge crop of Irishers—excuse me, "Hiberni-ans," as they like to call themselves. Somebody said there's even a German or two although nobody can name them.

I guess they had some shakeups in Europe about ten years ago. Nothing like our revolution or the big one in France that followed. Still, there was a lot of yelling and a few things got broken, and people decided that it was better anyplace else than where they were.

Mike said France started it by tossing out an emperor, but they messed it up by electing the same guy as president. Then, after they settled down a bit, he became emperor again.

This is not the way to run a revolution, if you ask me. And Mike said other countries over there were raising hell over conditions and aristocracies. He rattled off some names of countries but said he didn't know them. He'd never sailed there, places like Hungary or Poland.

People wanted more democracy. They fought and lost. Many of them left to come over here.

It makes me wonder, though. What if we look up some day, and there are lots more of them here than there are of us? I told that to Mike, and he gave me one of his straight-forward looks.

"The day that happens," he said, "you can appreciate how the Indians feel."

Boston has more Irish than Ireland, I believe, and they've been coming over in droves. The way people are leaving there, Ireland must be light enough to float. They had plenty of gripes against England, but they came crowding here for a different reason.

It's all because of a problem with potatoes. That seemed strange to me, at first, because although we eat potatoes at home, we could probably do without them. I mean, you can make chowder out of corn, too. But then I learned that potatoes are about all they ate. No kidding. Pounds of them, mostly boiled. Now I ask you, why would people who live on an island surrounded by the ocean have to live on potatoes? Why, we could live on what we catch, adding a little corn and beans to fill out the corners of our stomachs, and I didn't see why the Irish couldn't do the same.

Grandpa Mike says I don't understand that the British run things in Ireland, and they squeeze pretty hard. Sure, there's fishing, but if you don't have a dime, you can't buy a boat, and if you are off away from the coast grubbing out a bare existence on land belonging to somebody who doesn't care whether you live or die then you may not enjoy a balanced diet.

He told me that when they started coming over after the potatoes failed, they were in a sorry state, the men with gaunt faces and staring eyes, and the women and kids just barely able to walk ashore. Most of them were fed by the people they had contracted with to come over, but you know those steerage meals must have been awfully grim. Once they got here, most of them went to work, and within just five or six years were able to crawl back into some sort of a decent life, although not one I'd like to have.

The early Irish who had come across about forty years ago, when they were building the Erie Canal, had collected in New York and Boston and were getting big enough in politics to be heard. They helped the newcomers as long as the immigrants voted with them.

Mike told me that about the only thing that kept a lot of them alive back home was the ability to keep warm.

"It was all because of Pete," he said. Or that's what I thought he said.

"Who's Pete?"

"Not Pete—a name—but P-E-A-T. It's a wet turf that they cut off from the top of the ground. They dry it and use it in their stoves, if they have any, or fireplaces, if they don't."

"They dig it out of the ground and use it like firewood?"

"Yes. Sort of. And it has a nice smell."

Something new I learned about the Irish.

But they're still the target of a lot of jokes.

I told one to Grandpa Mike, and he said it was a dumb joke and that if I repeated it, I'd be dumb, too.

Since Mike didn't seem to want to talk about Irish jokes, I took a new tack and said I guessed the Irish are a lot smarter than I thought.

"Why do you say that?"

"They learned to burn dirt."

Mike sniffed. "Just because people arrived starving and in rags is no reason to think they're dumb," Grandpa Mike said. "Damned few of us came over here in silver sailboats."

"I still think some of the jokes are sort of funny," I said.

"I understand, and nobody really knows what makes something funny. For instance, if next winter you saw that stuck-up Burleigh boy walking down the street and suddenly he slipped on the ice and he landed on his ass, well, you'd think that was funny. I would too. But if Widow Chambers slipped the same way, carrying a basket of eggs that splattered all over the road, we wouldn't laugh at all. As I say, what's funny is a hard thing to pin down."

"Does the widow get hurt?"

"What kind of a question is that?"

"If she doesn't get hurt and just flips up in the air, her skirts over her head, and volleys eggs all over the place like grapeshot, I might laugh."

"You shouldn't. After all, you've got to show respect for the widow."

"So it isn't what happens, it's who it happens to that makes it funny?"

"Well, that's not always the case, Luke. Some things are funny because they're just so damned ridiculous that you have to laugh. There's a story about somebody—I can't remember who—who laughed himself to death watching a jackass trying to eat a pickle. I'm sure it looked ridiculous."

"I think it's pretty funny that he laughed himself to death watching the jackass."

"You can't be laughing at people dying."

"I guess if they're laughing when they do it, it's probably okay, Grandpa."

"Luke," he said, his ears getting red, "sometimes I think you just talk to annoy me."

With that he rose and stomped his way to the door.

"And I don't want to hear you laughing at me after I leave!"

But I'll bet he did.

## CHAPTER 7

LIKE THAT STUFF ABOUT WHAT IS AND ISN'T FUNNY, GRAND-pa likes to give me these lectures, and I guess they don't hurt anything. Sometimes, I even learn something. Most of what I know about the people in Marblehead came from him—all that about the Portugee and Irish and others who came here from somewhere else.

Mainly, though, as I said, most of them with English roots, and there have been quite a few English men and women coming over lately, like they wished they'd done it a long time ago. People here work at all kinds of things, some in the shoe factories and others are lawyers, judges, teachers, preachers, shopkeepers, women who sew quilts and clothes, sell candles or cakes, some fellows who work for the railroad, shipwrights and riggers, carpenters, people who own the fishing boats who don't sail, and some who own their own boats and do. Some own companies that sell the fish, and others just work for them. And then there are those who don't seem to do a damned thing but hang out around the docks, swill beer or whiskey, whittle, and spit tobacco. I've never figured out how they get by, at all. Maybe I'm missing something.

Also, for years, New England has been booming in the cloth business, or textiles, as they say. From what I hear, there's not a farm in Maine, New Hampshire, Vermont, or Massachusetts that doesn't have at least one daughter who has worked in a mill someplace. Every little river or stream has been dammed to get water power for the big looms. The women who work in these places look as washed-out as the cloth. You don't see many pink cheeks when they come out the doors at the end of the day. But I guess they are making a living, a poor one, sure enough. Now, it's slowed but may be getting better.

A few years back, when I was just a little kid about six years old, there was that big noise about gold in California I told you about, and some people went nuts. Men who you'd think had a good grip on things suddenly took off for the gold fields. "California Fever," people called it. But off they went to someplace in Missouri, buying wagons and stocking them with flour, bacon, pots, pans, and blankets; or sailing around the Horn to get there; or going down to a place called Panama and taking a mule train over to the Pacific Ocean. And what they found wasn't pots of gold, and most never even got a pot to put under the bed. Or maybe they didn't have a bed, either, and were busted before they got out of San Francisco. They acted crazy when they got there. Ships that had cost a fortune to build and crew clogged San Francisco harbor and just sat there because nobody could be found to sail them back. Hundreds of them. A lot of the fortune hunters stayed there and became farm workers, carpenters, cooks, and who knows what, and others came drifting back here, flat broke and disillusioned. Every now and then another one washes up in Marblehead, full of lies about the strike he made and lost, or else he just stares off into space and says nothing. The problem with illusions, I guess, is that it's probably better to get rid of them at home before you haul them halfway around the world to discover that you can't eat them.

The California gold rush was something of a blessing for us here, though. It opened up a whole new supply of hides from California, Mexico, and some places down in South America. They pack them in ships the way you'd stack lumber, and they are so hard they have to be soaked and treated for days before anybody can do anything with them. There's a book that tells about how they got California hides before the gold rush really opened up the trade. It's called *Two Years Before the Mast*, and it isn't a jokebook, for sure. The man who wrote it is a big Boston lawyer now, named Dana. He was the same fellow who stepped in a couple of years back to represent an escaped slave named Anthony Burns who had been tracked down by his owner who came all the way up from Virginia to get him back.

That set off a ruckus in Boston, and one policeman got killed in the riot. It turns out that you can be a free black man or woman in Massachusetts but not in Virginia, and if you come here from there to be with other free black men and women, they can still claim you back there as a slave. That doesn't seem right to me. Besides, why should a man be free or a slave just because he lives someplace or other? We don't get to pick where we're born, do we?

Might as well say that we could have free black men and slave white men up here, just to balance things out. I sure don't want anybody owning me. It's bad enough just being a kid.

This whole slave thing has been rubbing lots of folks in New England the wrong way, and some people are talking about a war if things don't change. I don't suppose that would affect us much, though. We're a long way from Virginia or South Carolina. If there is a war, I'll bet I'll be in it—if it lasts long enough.

# { CHAPTER 8 }

THE FIRST THING I READ TO THE SHOEMAKERS, AND IT WAS as much for me as for them, was the Lambs' *Tales from Shakespeare*, all the stories from the plays but without all the fancy language. It's not so much that Shakespeare's words are puffed up, but they sure can muddy the line of the story. Just to give you an example, take that place in *Henry V*, where he tosses in this line:

"I'll fer him, and firk him, and ferret him."

Now, I ask you, just what in hell does that mean? I went to the school dictionary, but it didn't help. And I really like the story! It's a corker, if you can just get through the other stuff.

The same thing goes for *Macbeth* and *Othello*, and some of the others, but I've got to say that a lot of it comes down to that line in *Julius Caesar* where he says, "For mine own part, it was Greek to me." And that's why the Lambs did us all a good turn. Maybe later I can plow through the original stories a little easier, but I'm afraid I'm going to have to sweat it.

I'll bet you haven't heard the joke about the Lambs' book. A kid goes to a really stupid bookseller and says he'd like the Lambs' *Tales*, and the bookseller says he should go to a butcher shop. Ez told me that, and I laughed and laughed.

I guess some people say what Shakespeare wrote is poetry, but I'm not sure about that. I think a poem ought to rhyme, and Shakespeare doesn't do much of that. He wrote some things called sonnets that do rhyme, only I haven't really spent time with them, yet. I looked at a couple of them, but they seem to be a lot of love mush. Besides, I'm a little shy about getting involved with poetry, but I'll tell you about that later.

Last year was really tough for the shoemakers. People said there was a "panic" in the country, something going wrong with money and jobs and imports and exports—I don't pretend to know much about these things. It hit us all pretty hard and all the shoe factories shut down and put the workers out. Well, not all—Joseph Bassett kept his factory on Prospect Street going, and that fed several hundred families. But Harris closed, and so did Haskell, and their workers wouldn't have made it except that Bassett hired nearly all of them. I don't know how he did it. Was he still making money during that time? If he was, why weren't the others? And if he wasn't, how did he keep on paying them? Maybe he was like old Moses Pickett, who died about five years ago. Nobody seemed to like old Mose, called him stingy and mean, said he could squeeze a dollar so hard the eagle screamed, but after he died, they read his will and found that he'd left a house to be used for widows, and thirteen thousand dollars to pay for them and the upkeep of the property. With all the ship losses at sea over the years, there's a big supply of widows and orphans and no money coming in.

Only after he was dead did people come forward and tell about how old Mose used to dole out money to widows, sick old people, and kids who had no fathers, like me, except I had people who could take care of me. And merchants and shopkeepers said that Mr. Pickett had given them money so that they could offer free food and clothes to poor folks, but they had to swear that they'd keep secret what he did.

Sometimes, you think that most people in the world should be walked off the end of a pier, and then there's a Pickett to make you reconsider.

The panic that hit the shoemakers also hit businesses all over New England, and lots of men have been trooping around looking for work. I don't know what the girls and women did. I suppose the ones who lost their jobs just went back to the farm. We don't have enough boats to hire landsmen on for fishing. We can't even keep our own fishermen busy all the time. And when people are out of work, they don't buy as much of anything as they do when they have some coins to jingle, and that includes fish. It's a good thing we can dry the cod because if the Marbleheaders had to sell all their fish fresh off the boat, they'd be in a pickle. The Marbleheaders, not the fish. Nobody around here likes pickled fish. The worst of the cod goes down to the Caribbean where they'll eat anything, I guess.

Things seem to be a little easier these days, with some of the shoe factories starting up again and the little shops hiring workers. I like to joke to myself that they hire them for me to read to, but I know that's not the case.

Most of the workers want me to read books or stories, and I feel the same way. When I first started reading to them, almost three years ago, I wasn't as good as I am now, and my level of stories was pretty low. Now, though, I can tackle just about anything from Sir Walter Scott and Washington Irving to Pope's poetry—not the Pope, Alexander Pope—and even that guy who wrote about the white whale. That one almost put the workers to sleep, and they asked me not to read them any more of his stuff.

And somebody wanted me to read a book by another Massachusetts fellow, Hawthorne is his name, from Salem. And this was about a woman and a preacher and how they made a baby, even though they weren't married, and how she and her kid, a little girl named Pearl, were forced to live apart from all the rest of the folks in the town, and the woman had the letter *A* embroidered on her dress. I never figured that one out, but Piggy Waller, one of the guys at school, said he thought it meant she was "Adulterated." Maybe so. The workers seemed to follow it, and some of the women snuffled over their sewing while they worked. The story gets confusing: This woman was married to an old man in England, she took up with this preacher over here, and Salem, which was run by those Puritan people, treated her like dirt. The preacher wouldn't own up to his part in the deal, and later he has apoplexy, or something, and dies. When they opened his shirt, they found a big red *A* burned on his chest. Piggy said it probably stood for "arsehole," and I had to agree.

It made me understand how politicians do their business: you don't have to know what you're saying for people to get all worked up over it.

The story wouldn't have worked in Gloucester. Those

women over there are a pretty ready bunch and would have told the Puritans to go piss up a lightning rod.

This reading's been good for me. I've learned a lot because of it, and it makes me feel a little more grown up to sit on a high stool by the window and reel off page after page while the workers stitch away, sometimes nodding their heads, sometimes shaking them, and sometimes even making loud comments about a character or his activities. I guess the people in these books are pretty close to the real thing, even though they're just made up. It's hard to imagine that a Becky Sharp could live in Marblehead, although some of the workers feel that they know somebody just like her.

Some of my schoolmates made fun of me when I first started reading in the shops and said I was putting on the dog, or trying to impress people. That wasn't it at all. I just liked doing it and like it even more now that I do it pretty well. I can't help it if some folks like to gabble over nothing, when if they'd spend a little time with their noses in books instead of those beer mugs, they'd learn a lot. Of course, folks don't need to know what they're talking about to spend all day making ignorant remarks. One oaf will start things off, then another will add his dumb thought, and a third will chime in with an equally dull comment, and they reach conclusions that wouldn't be fit for a three-year-old. You'd think that if you added several brains together, you'd be able to come up with some intelligence, but it doesn't always work that way.

After I've finished a book or just a story at one shop, I move to another so that I can read to as many of the shoemakers as possible. When I leave a shop after a week or so, you'd think I had been feeding them cakes instead of just words. The men clap me on the back and the women hug me and they all make me promise to come back when their turn comes around again.

In the summer, I don't read to them as much because my grandparents have more things for me to do, and, I guess I'm selfish here, I like to spend time reading by myself. It's more satisfying not having to listen to myself. When I read by myself, I hear the words in my head, and they sound just fine up there. Besides, with so much of the shoe business still on the skids, not many shops are begging to be entertained, at least not by me.

Maybe I should learn to sing.

## { CHAPTER 9 }

IF LAST YEAR WAS BAD, THE YEAR BEFORE WAS PRETTY GOOD.
We had a knockout Fourth of July, and you couldn't have
had a better one even in Boston, I'll bet. The whole town
looked like it had dressed ship, with flags and pennants
everywhere, kids with combed hair and shoes on, women
with ringlet curls down to their shoulders, and men stuffed
into suits that maybe used to fit. The plan was to go into
motion about nine o'clock in the morning, but some of the
officials had already kissed a jug from the way they were
frisking around, so we got off late. We had three military
companies, all tricked out in finery, the whole fire depart-
ment and their equipment was in line, and then the parade
began. Every former and present town official who could
make it was there, and there were carriages that rolled along
full of old people who couldn't march. We even had a bunch
of mounted men and some Indians on horseback, though
nobody ever heard of a troop of New England Indians riding horses. Every club, association, society, and whatnot had

dolled up in their best and walked in the parade. But the best thing was us: the kids from school.

All of the kids—the newspaper next day called us "scholars"—got to march along with the grown-ups. Ez and I had got some red, white, and blue bunting and tied it around Bugle's legs and neck, and we'd fixed a red flower on his tail. He was some sight! Do dogs ever go around bragging to other dogs about the way they look? Bugle surely could have. Ez dressed up like a pirate, although what that had to do with the Fourth of July I really can't say.

There were ladies trying to look like Columbia, with loose draping gowns and torches, but they were a lot more covered up than a couple of pictures of Columbia I had seen in Boston. We—Grandpa, Grandma and I—had gone into this big hall that had paintings hanging all over the walls. One room, more of a hallway really, led off the main room, and I wandered into it. It had pictures of men and women with no clothes on! Honest. One had two naked men wrestling. I think they were Romans or some really old-time guys. Another had these women in a big pool, like they were bathing, and they didn't have a stitch on! And the two Columbias had little spiky crowns around their heads, and neither one had enough sense to keep their gowns closed. Both of them had their top hamper hanging out, and either didn't notice or didn't care. You may not believe me, but it's true.

Grandma saw me in there and just about fainted. She screeched something, and Mike came in, trying to keep from laughing, and grabbed me by the arm and hustled me out. Grandma lifted her chin up and walked out of the place like she'd been starched. Mike just pulled me along and gave me a wink. I have a feeling they're not going to take me back there.

A couple of years back, an older boy was kicked out of school for drawing pictures of women who were naked. Now, I only saw one, and it was just the back of a woman who was standing on a rock looking out to sea. As far as I could tell, it was as good as some of the stuff in that Boston gallery, but the folks who run the Marblehead school thought the Devil had taken possession of the town's youth, so the fellow was booted out the door. I heard that he went down to New York where they don't care whether women wear clothes and is making a living as a portrait painter. Funny thing, though: Was he an artist here, or just a kid drawing dirty pictures? And how do you know? And does it make any difference? And who were the women he drew? Are they still around town?

But I was telling you about the Fourth, and how everybody got decked out in some kind of showy outfits. There must have been a few open kegs because more than just the officials were stumbling over the paving by the time the festivities really got started. You saw normally staid gentlemen in knee britches and buckled shoes, their hair done up like George Washington and Benjamin Franklin, slapping each other on the back and laughing at nothing. If they were supposed to be acting like the Founding Fathers, the country must have had a pretty shaky start.

It went on for a long time, almost all day, in fact. After the parade downtown, we all went to the Old North Church for a speech by some windbag—God! Some of these guys could wear down a brick wall—and there were prayers, too. You can't walk in a church just to get out of the sun without somebody heading into a prayer. Then the choir sang an "Ode" that one of their members had written, and it wasn't much in the musical line, at least, I didn't think so. But the reading of the Declaration of Independence came off all right, those words rolling out over the crowd and a little shiver running up my back when we got to "our lives and our sacred honor." We were all pretty familiar with the Declaration, but it still got to us, I think.

That night we had fireworks. And there's nothing prettier than those flares and rockets and the stars in the sky, and all of it reflected in the waters of Marblehead Harbor. I guess you could say we're proud of the way we celebrate the Fourth.

Last year, in New York, they had riots like you wouldn't believe, with gangs going at each other with knives, iron bars, and even guns. People got killed, and a lot got hurt, and all because somebody thought he and his group should tell everybody else what they should do. Seems like that's the reason we had the Revolution in the first place and why we have the Fourth of July.

I wish I'd been around for some of the other big doings here in town, like when George Washington came to Marblehead to thank the men for their help in pulling him out of the mess he got himself into with the British on Long Island. Those were Marbleheaders who rowed his army across to safety. And they were there to row him and his troops across the Delaware, so he had good reason to come to town and tell them he appreciated what they did. His ass would likely have been in a British jail if it hadn't been for them.

The best one must have been when the Marquis—the French say "Markee"—visited here about thirty-five years ago. Grandpa Mike was a boy then and said it was a real rip-snorter. The Marquis, which was his title, and I guess it was a pretty big job, had the last name of Lafayette, and he'd been one of Washington's aides during the Revolution. They had a big dinner for him at the Hooper mansion or the Lee Mansion or one of those huge houses, and people cheered him all over town. There's a house on the hill that has one corner knocked off so that the second floor juts out over the street, but there's nothing on the first floor. People say the corner was removed so that the Marquis's coach could make it around the corner, and I guess that would have been a good idea because it's a right sharp turn. But Grandpa Mike says the corner had been taken off earlier to make room for wagons with drunken drivers that kept running into the house. I don't suppose it makes much difference. Besides, a good story is sometimes worth shaving an edge off the truth.

My own view is that the wagon drivers weren't drunk but that their horses were stupid. I never met a horse that wasn't. If there's one sure thing not to count on in this world, I'd say it was a horse's brain. It must be about the size of a minnow's. I'll admit that I don't have much to do with horses. They're just around—big and strong and unpredictable. They rear up and throw their riders for no reason that anybody can see, they kick, and they sometimes bolt down the road pulling a little two-wheel rig with some terrified old man in it, or they step on your foot. They do other things like cover the streets with manure—I'll bet there's not a pair of shoes or boots in any town in the country that doesn't have horseshit on them—and they seem to host every fly in the universe, but those are just for starters. I guess they behaved well enough when the Markee made his visit. He managed to leave here alive.

When Andy Jackson came to town, he didn't even stay for dinner.

{ CHAPTER }
# 10

I STILL HAVEN'T DECIDED WHAT I WANT TO DO WHEN I grow up, although I imagine that it will have to do with boats some way or another. I know I could work for my Grandpa, like I do now, only full time and with pay, but I don't know how that would play. I want to see a lot more things than just around Marblehead, even though I could be in a lot worse place. When Mike and Grandma Ellen get really old, somebody's got to be around to look after them, and I guess that will be me. Still, they're both pretty lively right now, and they should wear well for another few years, and that could give me some time to go off on my own. I mean, Mike did, didn't he? Of course, his family was all gone by the time he went sailing. Even so, I'll bet that if they'd had these big clippers when he was younger he'd have jumped on one as quick as a bird on a worm, and he surely won't try to keep me from signing on in a couple of more years. I mean, China, for God's sake! Me on a clipper! Well, that's down the line a bit, and even if they don't seem to be building the really fast ones these days, there'll have to be some kind of clippers around. So what if I haven't made up my mind about the future? I know I want to see what's on the other side of the ocean.

Mr. Foster, Agatha's father, he's a lawyer, says I should read for the law, but I don't know about that. He lives in a big house in town, and it appears that being a lawyer brings in a lot of money, although he never gets to go anywhere much. Most of his time is spent looking at papers and into books, which would be all right if they were interesting, and, I have to admit, some of them are. There was a case I was reading in his office one day about a family that was suing some undertaker because a corpse, the grandfather in the family, I believe, had been put in a lead-lined coffin because they all thought that it would keep him until the trumpet sounds. The undertaker had a different way of keeping the bodies fresh, so to speak, and rigged a pump to pull all the air out of the coffin and sealed it with a lead plug. Well, I guess there was enough air in there for the grandfather to get pretty ripe, and at the funeral, with all the mourners sitting right in the front pew of the church, the plug blew and the smell just drove everybody outside.

If all the cases were that much fun, I'd be more interested in lawyering. Most of them seem to be pretty dry, though.

Mr. Foster has a lot of books that don't have anything to do with the law. Some are about philosophy, whatever that really is. I haven't figured it out yet, mainly because there doesn't seem to be just one of them, philosophy, that is, and everybody from the Greeks to the Germans and the French wade in and pronounce that they've got the ticket. It's sort of like religion, I guess. In Marblehead, we've got all kinds of churches: Episcopal, Baptist, about three Congregational, and now the Catholics are building one of their own. And, to hear them tell it, each one is right. Grandpa says that's fine with him, as long as they leave him alone. He says he went to a couple of them where everybody was told that they were miserable sinners and worthless human beings.

"I may go once to hear somebody tell me I'm worthless, but I'm damned if I go back to hear it again."

But he can get grumpy about anything.

Mr. Foster has history books, too, and I get a kick out of them. Some are almost as dry as the law books, but some have some exciting stuff, as well. The only problem I have is that there's not one book of all history—of course it's because there's just so much of it—but it would be nice to be able to pick up a book and read straight through all the things that have happened to people instead of trying to piece together what followed what from one book to another. You can learn that the Persians and Greeks had big civilizations, then there's a gap, and the Romans come along. They get thumped by the Vandals and the Goths, and there's a jump to the Turks, but you've also got the Mongols razing everything from China to Budapest, and we don't know much of anything about them.

I asked Mr. Foster about the Mongols, and he said there wasn't much of a record.

"They were led by a great warrior named Genghis Khan," he said. "He was the scourge of the earth, in those days, and his mounted army swept out of Central Asia and conquered everything in its path."

"And they didn't write about it? Leave a record?"

"We have only fragments of historical accounts, which is somewhat surprising seeing that they opened up the East to Europe—and the other way around. We know that after Genghis Khan, his grandson Kublai Khan took over leadership and became emperor of China. Eventually the Mongol horde faded back into Asia leaving only scraps of writing—orders, proclamations, official journals, that sort of thing, straightforward, factual material. And most of what we know was written by those they had conquered. The Mongols, as far as I know, had no poetry at all."

"Well," I said, "I guess we shouldn't judge them too harshly for that. They had their prose and Khans."

He gave me a startled look that wasn't quite a smile. More like he was going to ask a question but decided not to.

# { CHAPTER 11 }

I GOT TO BE SORT OF FRIENDS WITH MR. FOSTER BECAUSE his daughter, Agatha, is one of my schoolmates. I like her, I guess, even though she's the reason I had my only fight. Oh, I've had a couple of other pushing matches and that sort of thing but never a real scrap with anybody until the day Tommy Drew opened his mouth when he should have kept it closed.

You see, Agatha is a really pretty girl, I think, and she's not stuck up one bit, but she has one little defect, or so some people think. One of her eyes is just a little bit off course. Not much, I tell you, and you only notice it when you are directly in front of her and she's looking straight at you, or would be except for that eye. Of course, she almost never does that and turns her head ever so slightly so that you can't tell that both eyes aren't aimed in the same direction. Personally, I think it's kind of interesting because you never know exactly which way she's looking and whether she's looking at you or just past you. And they're dark brown with sort of hazel rings around them.

Anyway, we had all walked down to the center of town after school and were fooling around, not doing much of anything when Agatha said she had to get home and took off for her house. I was standing there watching her go when Tommy Drew said:

"She's kind of good-looking for a cross-eyed girl."

That just got me riled and I told him to take it back. Anybody who is cross-eyed is suspected of bringing bad luck on board ship, of being a Jonah, and I wasn't about to let Tommy get away with saying something bad about her. Besides, just as I said, she wasn't really that way at all.

"What, the good-looking girl part or the cross-eyed part?"

"You know damn well what part!"

"Don't you swear at me," he said, shoving me backward with both hands.

I slapped them away and he took a swing at me with his right fist. Like when a boom swings across the deck on a gybe, if you notice it, you can get your head down. If you don't, you can have your brains spattered. I saw Tommy's fist coming and ducked underneath, then hit him full in the stomach with my own right hand.

He made a sound like "Ooh-n-n-n!" and started stumbling backward, like he was running on his heels but not doing a very good job of it. He stuck one of his feet in a rain bucket that was standing on the walk outside the dry goods shop and fell down in the water. Then he started to squall, and I was afraid that I'd really hurt him. But he jumped up, doubled over holding his stomach, and lit out for home bawling that he'd tell his brother on me.

Maybe he did, but his brother never said anything about it

to me, and, for sure, Tommy never made any more remarks about Agatha's eyes. I heard later that the reason he ran home holding his stomach wasn't because he was hurt but because when he fell he popped off his suspender buttons and was trying to hold his pants up.

Well, as I say, it was because of Agatha that I got to know Mr. Foster, and it's a good thing I did because he saved me from a miserable situation that I got myself into. It wasn't as though I did anything bad, but my teacher, a chilly old man, Mr. Elias Seeger, tried to make me sound like I was a traitor, and he called me an "insufferable whelp" and a couple of other things that he shouldn't have. And, naturally, being the kind of schoolmaster he was, he wanted to beat me with his cane. That was not in the master plan of the universe, as far as I was concerned.

The way it came about was that Mr. Seeger told us all to write a poem about the American Revolution. He talked about it as though he had been at the head of every company of soldiers that faced the redcoats. Everything was glamorous in his eyes, and he barely mentioned that anyplace but New England took part in the conflict. It was Concord, this, Lexington, that, Bunker Hill, and just about every scuffle that occurred in the area. But he shortchanged the rest of the colonies, I thought, and you had to look hard in the history books to learn that many battles took place down south, and that Washington led his troops in New Jersey, Pennsylvania, and, finally, down on his home ground of Virginia, where Lord Cornwallis gave up. If Mr. Seeger had his way, he'd have left us all thinking the surrender took place on the Back Bay.

Well, I guess I was full of vinegar about then—I was younger at the time—because I wrote a poem and handed it in. It's not a great poem. I'm not really a poet, although I was put off by Mr. Seeger's attitude and thought I'd fire off a round. I should have had better sense.

Anyway, here's what I wrote:

We've heard about heroes at Concord,
Of Boston, and all of that tea.
We've learned that the British
Became rather skittish,
And looked for their safety at sea.

But in all of the stories they tell us,
Of battles waged both near and far,
The only brave legions,
Seemed to come from these regions,
And New Englanders won the whole war!

Which causes me problems aplenty,
When looking at maps late at night,
New Jersey saw action,
New York had a fraction,
But New Englanders won the whole fight!

Valley Forge isn't found in New Hampshire,
Monmouth's not 'neath a Rhode Island star,
Pennsylvania bled,
And Virginia ran red,
But New Englanders won the whole war!

Perhaps as a generous gesture,
We might recognize comrades in arms,

From the Hudson's north reaches
To Caroline's beaches,
And Georgia's plantations and farms.

There's honor enough for the country
We need not be stingy and mean,
In praising the glory,
Let's tell the whole story,
New England's just part of the scene.

I wrote it all out and handed it in with the rest of the class
poems. Mr. Seeger smiled his thin-lipped grimace and started flipping through the pile. Suddenly, he straightened his
back, his face coloring to a bright crimson.

"You there! You, Lucas!"

I cringed, but stood up as we are supposed to do when
our names are called.

I guess you're not surprised to learn that my first name
is Lucas, not Luke, but that day it didn't matter.

"This is outrageous!" he yelled. "You are not worth one
one-thousandth of any Minute Man or any gallant soldier
in the Continental Army. You are a scoundrel!"

I was petrified. Old Seeger was blazing and looked as if
he'd explode any second. I cut a glance at Agatha, sitting in
the front row—all the girls sat in the front row—and her
face was the color of a scarlet maple. I didn't know whether
she was angry with me or with Mr. Seeger or just embarrassed at both of us. I didn't like the names he was calling
me, but I could take them all right. What I didn't fancy was
him whacking my backsides with his cane just because I had
some ideas that were not precisely the same as his.

"Come here and take your caning, you miserable whelp!"

"Mr. Seeger, sir. May I ask what I've done?"

"What have you done? You little wretch, you have dared to hand in this unnatural and unpatriotic doggerel, that's what you have done!"

"I'm sorry, Mr. Seeger, but I think it's very patriotic. It recognizes all the heroes of the Revolution."

"I'm not here to debate your misbegotten verse. Get up here and take your punishment!"

I'd never seen him so upset. Really out of his mind. Still, I thought he was unfair and that all I had done was follow his instruction to write a poem about the Revolution. And it was that Revolution that gave me the right to say what I thought. My next mistake was to say that to Mr. Seeger.

"Damn your eyes!" he bellowed.

The cane was whipping about.

"Get up here and take a thrashing!"

"I don't think I will, Mr. Seeger. I think I'm leaving here now. I have no reason to be caned for something I wrote that tells the truth as best I know it. I'm going home." And I did.

## CHAPTER
{ 12 }

WHEN I GOT HOME, GRANDMA ELLEN WAS STARTLED TO see me in the middle of the morning when I was supposed to be at school. She listened to my side of the story, then got her shawl and walked me down to the chandlery to see my Grandpa. He wasn't there. Somebody had ordered some parts for a ship up in Salem, and he had left for up there an hour earlier, according to Willie Howells, the handyman who worked in the yard next door.

We were standing in front of the shop, Grandma trying to decide what to do next, when Mr. Foster walked our way.

"Good day to you both," he said, lifting his tall beaver hat.

"And a good day to you, sir," Grandma answered.

"Why, Lucas, I'm surprised to see you," he said.

"Yes, sir."

"Did school let out today? I hadn't heard about it."

"No, sir. School's in. I'm out."

At that point, Grandma began telling Mr. Foster what had happened, and he seemed very interested in what she was saying. He looked at me from time to time, but he wasn't getting red in the face the way old Seeger—Mr. Seeger—did.

"Do you remember the poem?" Mr. Foster asked me.

I admitted that I did.

"Recite it for me."

In for a penny. So, I reeled it off and kind of enjoyed having an audience. When I finished, Mr. Foster sort of laughed and said, "I don't see treason there. It might even be considered a corrective measure."

Then he looked at Grandma Ellen with a twinkle in his eye and said, "Leave him to me."

Mr. Foster took me by the arm, and we walked up the hill toward the schoolhouse. As we approached, we could hear the voices of the younger students droning out their multiplication tables in a ragged chorus. This was historic. No adults ever came to the school during class time, but here was Mr. Foster, a well-known, prosperous citizen bringing me up to the schoolhouse door. We stood in the doorway for a moment until Mr. Seeger noticed that the pupils were looking our way. He obviously didn't understand what was happening, apparently thinking that a leading member of the community had collared and returned a truant.

Hurrying over to the doorway, his hands washing each other as he came, he gave a curt bow to Mr. Foster and glared at me.

"You'll get twice as many stripes for running away, you rascal!"

"Hold there, Mr. Seeger," Mr. Foster cut in. "Young Lucas, here, has told me about your assignment and has recited his poem for me. I quite like it. Nothing great in the poetry line, no doubt, but it shows that here in Marblehead we teach a broader view of history than, say, what goes on in Cambridge where they think the world revolves around them. As his teacher, you must congratulate yourself on your perception of the events of the Great Revolution and how it was the concerted effort of many people from many backgrounds who eventually forced the Crown to give us our freedom."

Mr. Seeger stood dumbstruck. He didn't know which way to jump.

Mr. Foster went on: "There are some people, alas, in this wonderful republic who fail to understand what that word 'freedom' means. But we understand it, don't we, Mr. Seeger? We've read the Constitution and the Bill of Rights and we know that the freedom to think, to entertain all sorts of ideas, is not just a whim of someone who holds momentary authority over the people. That's why they are called 'Rights,' Mr. Seeger. Anything else would be tyranny, and we'd have to fight all over again. But, of course, you know all that. Rights are not handed down by men but are what we are born with. I know you agree. You treasure all these things, and, obviously, you teach them, else young Lucas here wouldn't have known that he had the right to express himself."

Mr. Seeger made a noise. I don't know whether he was trying to talk or was just choking.

"At any rate, Mr. Seeger, those of us who value the education of our children always like to know how they are being taught. So, comfortable in the knowledge that you are a man of generous instincts who seeks only to expand the horizons of our young people, I'll feel free to question my daughter, Agatha, about the manner in which you go about this important task."

With that, Mr. Foster bade us another "Good day," and walked down the hill, leaving me with Mr. Seeger, a blank, staring, limp sort of man. He put one hand to the side of his face and slowly passed it across his eyes. As if noticing me for the first time, he said, "Lucas, what are you doing outside? Come in, boy. We've finished with poetry."

And we had. Agatha gave me a big smile, and the cane stood in the corner.

The way I tell it, you'd think I was proud of what I had done, but actually I felt bad about it, later. Sure, old Seeger shouldn't have threatened me with that cane, and he was wrong to put everything on New England's part in the Revolution, but he could have been a lot worse in what he taught, and I didn't appreciate that at the time. I thought I was pretty slick in writing that poem and only slowly came to realize that it was a smart-aleck thing to do. If it hadn't been for Mr. Foster, no telling where it would have wound up.

One day, after I had walked Agatha home from school, Mr. Foster came out of his front door and joked with her for a minute or two. She went inside and I started off down the street.

"Just a moment, Lucas."

I turned to see Mr. Foster strolling after me. He was a big man, and he looked something like Agatha, although I think people see too much resemblance in relatives most of the time. Particularly with babies who all look alike to me.

"I wanted to talk to you about that rhyme you wrote."

"It wasn't much, really."

"I think you're right. It was verse, of a sort, to be sure, but it wasn't poetry by any standards I know."

I could feel my stomach sinking.

"You're a clever young chap and seem to have read a good deal. However, there's much more to the art of poetry than just stringing words together and having the end of the line rhyme with the one ahead of it. That's one thing about the law: nobody who works with lawbooks confuses what he reads with poetry."

"Yes, sir." I was sort of humiliated by then. "I wouldn't have tried any poem at all except that Mr. Seeger told us we had to write something."

"Yes. Well, I doubt that a classroom assignment ever produced a real poem, so don't feel too bad about it. I gather that you won't be challenging your teacher after this."

"Mr. Foster, if I was told to write a poem about the Revolution ever again, I'd try as hard as I could to glorify the home folks, but I still can't come up with a good rhyme for 'Boston,' or 'Concord,' or 'Lexington.' And 'Bunker Hill' just stops me cold. Maybe New England just isn't the spot for poetry."

Mr. Foster put back his head and laughed. "You may be right, Lucas. You may be right. And by the way, young man, if you go down to Virginia, you'll find that they think they won the war by themselves."

He put me to work reading some English poetry, fellows named Coleridge, Wordsworth, Byron, Shelley, and Keats. What a bunch of jackasses. Coleridge was a dope addict; Wordsworth went over to France, got a young woman pregnant, then scuttled back to England leaving her and the baby there; Byron seems to have been involved with boys, girls, men, and women, and bragged about a lot of it; Shelley ran off and married a sixteen- or seventeen-year-old girl, dropped her, and took up with another about the same age. Oh, he was a gentleman. After the first wife committed suicide, he married the one he was living with. She, by the way, wrote *Frankenstein*, maybe the worst book I ever groaned through.

But Keats was just a plain young fellow who paddled too far into the fog. He said that "Beauty is truth, truth beauty," and that's all we need to know. This may explain why poets starve. He died very early but not before turning out some wearisome stuff. Mr. Foster gave me a copy of a thing called "Endymion," and it nearly fried me. It goes on and on about this guy wandering through strange places having visions of women who come to make him happy, then disappear. This is pretty much it until you get near the end when he tosses in a thing called "The Indian Maiden's Roundelay," which, as far as I can tell, has absolutely nothing to do with the rest of the yarn.

The Indian maid is sad and sorrowful when suddenly music and noise are heard. It's the Greek god Bacchus—a young version, pulled in a chariot, accompanied by a covey of damsels and followed by a troupe of satyrs. Satyrs, of course, are supposed to do nothing much but ravish damsels, except they aren't doing that here.

We find out why when the Indian maid asks them:

> "Why have you left your forest haunts?
> Why left your nuts in oak tree cleft?"

Good God! These aren't satyrs. They're neutyrs.

That's when I closed the book.

{ CHAPTER }
# 13

As far as the boat was concerned, I was allowed considerable responsibility, but the business end of things was beyond me. Grandpa Mike had taken the train into Boston and wouldn't be back until tomorrow. Something about money, probably. He seldom went into the city unless it had to do with money, although I'm never sure whether he's depositing it, withdrawing it, borrowing it, or lending it. He goes around to big supply houses and banks and is on the lookout for anything new that his customers might want.

Usually, he spends the night there after one of these days, and every now and then he takes me and Grandma Ellen with him. That's a treat. We have dinner in a restaurant where they know him, and we stay at an inn. I guess if you had to live in a big city, Boston wouldn't be the worst, but I'll take Marblehead every time.

But something different has been going on these days. Not just the threat of nasty weather forecast by every barometer in the harbor and the mare's tail is up high in the sky twisting around almost in a circle, and not just the number of people who can't find work. Only yesterday I'd overheard Mike talking to some of the other men around the docks and caught the words "We'd better be on guard." The others had nodded in agreement, a few of them looking angry and edgy. When I asked what they had been talking about, the old man merely mumbled, "Some riffraff up to no good. It won't bother us."

Of course, I really shouldn't call him an old man. I'll have to give him that. When I was born, my mother was only twenty, and Grandpa Mike had just been twenty-two when she came along. Even so, there was plenty of gray hair in that mess of blue-black that covered his head, and my age now means that he has to be past fifty.

Grandpa Mike works pretty hard, just like anyone else who makes a living with a sailboat, but nobody thinks anything of it, and they just go about the business without much complaining. Everybody says that steam is going to be the end of sail for us and all the rest of the world. Steam packets are running on schedules that sailboats just can't meet—they don't much care which way the wind is blowing—and the passenger trade is nearly all gone to steam. Of course, those people who are putting all their money on steamboats are looking over their shoulders at the railroads, hauling people at a faster clip than any boat can do. Both boats and railroads are stuck with similar problems: they can only work if there's water or a track. The only better way would be to fly over places, but that's not likely to happen unless somebody can put a harness on an awful big bird.

Besides, sailboats are about the prettiest useful things that a man ever made. Nobody ever accused a railroad locomotive of being beautiful, and no carriage—even the ones with all kinds of doodads and gold paint—can compare with a big clipper with full canvas out. Why, a little cat boat gliding over the water beats all the buildings, steeples, and houses I've ever seen, and as for the *Mary Constance*, well, I admit to being sort of slanted in my view, but she's a beauty to me. And with her name all tricked out in gold paint on the stern—I painted the board myself—she's just a dandy. And when I go out to board her, it's always special.

The little black schooner with sun-bleached decks—black outside, except for the buff colored spars, all white inside—rocks slightly, hunting a bit as it tends slowly back and forth at its mooring, for it stays at a mooring and not at the dock.

Mike had got hold of a new kind of anchor that looks like an upside-down mushroom and which stays down all the time. A tar-sealed keg floats on an attached chain that runs to the anchor, settled deep in the mud. I'd tied our little dory off at the stern after I had rowed out.

As always, the small sounds of the planks working and the rigging swaying made the boat seem alive, though now and then it groaned as if it might like to break loose, freed for at least a day from the wearisome chores imposed by Grandpa Mike who drove the boat up and down the coast to Manchester, Lynn, Gloucester, Plymouth, Provincetown, and the rest, delivering small items from the chandlery to other sailors and fishermen who couldn't take time off from their own jobs to come to Marblehead. The idea of ship-to-ship delivery had been Mike's own and was not only profitable in itself, but it brought more business for the chandlery when appreciative customers came to Marblehead on other matters.

A couple of other men had tried to do the same thing, but they also carried coal, and that's something Grandpa wouldn't do.

"If I wanted to run a damned coal barge, I'd have built one," he said.

Which makes me snicker when he lugs coal aboard for his own stove. He has a small bunker set aside for the coal, and, much as he tries, it's impossible to keep the dust from seeping out into the cabin.

"Luke!" he'll yell. "Get moving and sweep up this cabin. I'm not running a coal barge, you know."

Grandpa also had one locker that held a few small bolts of cloth—flannel, calico, linen, things like that—and a few ribbons and some frilly stuff that women hang on themselves. All this was wrapped in butcher's paper and was for the wives of the other captains who figured it was going to make things easier at home if they could show up with something the ladies thought was pretty. Grandma Ellen doesn't go in much for frippery, but I know she enjoys getting little things to dress up with, and Mike never fails to bring some little trinket or piece of cloth back from his Boston visits.

Perhaps I should have stayed home with her today. Lots of times I help out in the kitchen, particularly when she's making something like an apple slump. She makes the dough and lets it rise, and I peel and core the apples before slicing them and putting them in the center of the dough ring she places in the round pan. One or the other of us pours on the molasses, and then we let it bake until she thinks it's ready. Boy, is that good! But not today. She has her jobs, and I have mine.

The boat is, by local standards, a new one, less than two

years old. Grandpa had her lines laid down years ago, changing them from time to time as new ideas would occur to him. He had an empty barn in which he stored the lumber he planned to use, letting it age until he was ready to use it. He picked out every plank himself and knew just where each one would go when the builders finally were to go to work. The hardware was cast in bronze, for the most part, each being squared with the overall design and with due consideration given to their weight. You can't just slap things on a really good boat without thinking about the fact that you are building something that moves in a world of water and that it must be stronger and more durable than any coach ever made. The added idea of having one that looks pretty is tied in with how it sails, and while there are some ugly boats for certain jobs, who would want to own one?

Some folks thought he never was going to build a boat, that it was just a dream he had that would be disturbed by reality. But there was a reason he started it and a reason he finished it. And a reason why he named it what he did.

Anyway, there I was in the warm and quiet up forward. I considered going on deck and practicing some splices with the marlinspike I got for my birthday, a real metal one, not one of those wooden fids that other kids had, but I already knew short and long splices and could do grommets and a couple of fancy knots if I had to. I closed the door separating the compartment from the saloon, making it like my private chamber, a secret hiding place. I figured I'd just rest there for a few minutes. Close my eyes. And....

## { CHAPTER 14 }

SOMETIMES IN MY DREAMS, I SAW MY FATHER. OR I GUESS I should say I believed it was my father. I could never put a complete face on the young man who seemed to live only when I was asleep. My father died when I was only a little more than two years old, so I couldn't be sure that the fellow who entered my dreams was anyone I knew. Perhaps it was only something my mind had made up from stories I'd been told about the things he did, the way he looked. Every so often I go up to Burial Hill where there's a tall monument, about fifteen feet high and made out of marble. You can see it from ten miles or so offshore because it's right on top of the hill. It's dedicated to the fishermen, my dad among them, who were lost at sea in the gale that struck the Banks, September 19, 1846.

That's what ruined the Marblehead fishing fleet. It says on the monument that it's a memorial to sixty-six men and boys, fifty-five heads of families, who left forty-three widows and more than one hundred fatherless children. I know a lot of those kids, of course, being one of them, all of us fatherless at one time, although some of the women have remarried. It hit us all at the same time, and that made us kin in a way, but—and I can't say why—we never talk about it to each other.

Lots of fishermen go out and never come back. That's just the way it is. Sometimes the sea takes the land folk as well. Just seven years ago, a big storm came bashing through here and all along New England, and people who thought they were safe on shore found their houses torn apart and drifting off on the sea. A couple of fellows, assistant keepers I think they were, were stuck out on the light at Minot's Ledge when the blow came up. The keeper had gone someplace ashore, looking for a skiff, as I remember it, because the one they used to get back and forth to the lighthouse had been beaten up. Minot's is a rough place to be.

So they had this lighthouse, a closed tower on top of some steel legs that stuck up about seventy feet or so over the ledge, and people who worked there complained that it swayed in high winds and seas and that it probably wasn't fit for the job. The people who ran the lighthouse business, especially the fellow who had the Minot's light built the way it was, said it was a fine lighthouse and would last for a hundred years. It had only been up about one.

You have to imagine what it was like: the ledge is about a mile offshore from Cohasset, and the lighthouse jutted up on its spidery legs with an egg-shaped housing on top for the light and the keepers. That Thoreau fellow, the writer, described it as looking like "an ovum of the sea," which is just another way of saying the same thing.

Well, the waves started building, and some were even

crashing against the windows of the tower, and the thing swayed and shook and finally came tumbling down. Both the assistant keepers were killed, although there was a story that one of them had actually managed to swim to Gull Island, but that he was so roughed up by the experience that he died after he made it ashore. How they figure that, I don't know. Any storm that could knock down a lighthouse and tear houses loose could easily wash an assistant keeper up the Bay and leave him on a rock. He wouldn't have to swim there.

They're building another one right now, out of huge blocks of stone. But Grandpa Mike says he'll probably be sitting in a rocking chair by the time they get it finished, although I have to say they've made a grand start and the blocks stand proud over the Ledge and look as if they could take a pounding. They'll have to. Lord, but that's a lonely-looking pile of rocks out there right now.

Of course, the main reason I go up to the Hill is that it's where my mother is buried. A simple white stone sits on her grave, with just her name, MARY CONSTANCE—you probably could have figured that out—and the dates of her short life. All around are headstones that are just crazy, as far as I'm concerned. Some are fantastic, carved with winged death's heads or skulls and crossbones or willow fronds. Some have inscriptions that are supposed to say something about those who are buried beneath. One, for a mother and her infant daughter, always puzzled me:

> TOO SWEET ALAS FOR MORTALS HERE
> THEIR SAVIOR CALLED THEM HOME.

I'd asked Grandpa Mike once to explain it, but all I got in

reply was a snort and a change of subject. As I've said, he isn't much for church-type stuff, and when my mother died, he tried to stay out of way of the church folks and looked over their heads if they caught him. One of the local preachers stopped him on the street one day and asked if he was ready for "The Awakening." Mike looked at him, smiled, and said he hadn't been asleep.

There's lots of people in the ground on the Hill, more young ones than old ones, it seems. I don't know why some people live so long and others barely stop by before they go. There's one old lady up there who lived into her nineties, but there are packs of little kids, some born dead and others who just made it for a couple of weeks. And, despite the old lady I mentioned, the women don't seem to last very long, many of them dying in their twenties and thirties—like my mom.

It's kind of interesting to see all those headstones up there. General Glover, one of George Washington's most valuable officers, and a bunch of his relatives are there, and several preachers, quite a few Revolutionary soldiers, and one of them was a fellow named Joseph Brown. The headstone says he was Marblehead's "Black Joe," and there's a pond up near the cemetery called "Black Joe Pond." I asked Mike if he was the one in the song, but he said he didn't think so.

Some of the old ladies around town think that I'm headed for damnation—I've heard them say so. They think Mike is raising me like a savage, and there's always somebody who just can't let other people live in a different way from themselves. Grandma Ellen, who is as good as anybody could be, won't listen to that kind of prattle, anyway. She just fixes her eyes on those biddies, and, like a flock of leghorns, they scuttle away, cackling as they go. I figured that Grandpa Mike and Grandma Ellen weren't going to let me go to hell if they had anything to do with it, and if there is one, so I just went along with what they asked me to do and tried to stay out of trouble. I don't do mean things, and I don't cheat, and I never lie—unless I have to—but some people think that the language I sometimes use is my ticket to perdition, even though I hear a lot worse from grown-up men around the docks and the shoeshops. If a bad word gets you dumped into hell, a lot of Marblehead's menfolk are going to be punching chunks down in that big boiler room someday.

Besides, you find these psalm-singers and prayer-meeting types all over the place who say "gosh darn" and "gol-danged" and "durn it to heck" and "doggone," and you know all they're doing is saying "God damn it" or "damn it to hell" but trying to disguise the words. If intention is what's going to be marked against you, they're in for a surprise, I guess.

I was part of one criminal thing. Just once. Some of the guys and I were loafing around one day, in July, I guess it was, because it was when the berry crop started coming in—and somebody got the idea that we should grab one of Mrs. Nichols's pies from her window sill. You see, Mrs. Nichols makes pies all the time, summer, winter, spring, and fall. Why she does that is anybody's guess. Her husband is a little wizened man who doesn't look as though he's ever had a full meal, much less a dessert. She gives some of the pies away, and she always comes up with something for her church socials and her sewing circle. Her rolling pin must be smoking from overuse. By any measure, I'd have to say that the output of pies at the Nichols house is impressive.

Now, I would never have thought about stealing one of her pies, and Ez wouldn't either, by himself, but when five or six others started clamoring for a raid on the Nichols' windowsill, our basic instincts simply disappeared. We didn't need a pie, and we weren't in the business of robbing people, yet we all agreed that it would be fun to lift one of Mrs. Nichols's efforts. I can't tell you why that was. Hell, if we'd been in New York, we might have tried to steal Mrs. Nichols. Anyway, her house was only a short way up the hill from where we were, and there were shrubs and a small stand of fruit trees behind it making the approach simple. We had enough sense not to go in a gang, but designated Ez to do the deed.

Ez is like a character out of a Fenimore Cooper book: tall, rangy, and smooth as a cat when he moves. He sidled up to the house, keeping just below the level of the windows, and surveyed the baking situation. Two blueberry pies, puffy and toasty brown on top, rested on the sill, cooling after having been taken out of the oven. Ez raised his right arm in a fluid motion and casually picked up one of the pies.

That's when his movements changed radically.

He had his thumb on the pie pan's rim and his fingers curled over onto the bottom. This, it turned out, was not the best example of how to grab a hot pie. She must have just put the pies on the sill because as soon as Ez firmed his grip, he felt a searing shot of pain and flung his arm involuntarily like one of those discus throwers you see in pictures about the Greeks or Romans. The pie tin sailed in a lazy arc across the Nichols' back yard and smacked into the side of a shed, painting the boards a lovely purple as the blueberries splattered. We split up and all took off as though the Old Nick was on our trail.

Afterward, after Ez had smeared his fingers with butter, he and I talked about what we had done and agreed that it was not only wrong, but stupid. He's not a lawbreaker and neither am I, and I don't think the other boys are either.

With his well-greased fingers pointing in the air, Ez asked me, "What the hell were we doing?"

"We, or you at any rate, were trying to nick a pie, and I think it's because one by one, we're all pretty honest, but once we got together, we couldn't wait to become crooks. When we put all of our consciences together, they didn't add more conscience. Maybe there's just something exciting about a bunch of guys busting the rules."

"That doesn't say much for getting people together," he said. "And besides, not all crooks work in groups, do they? Aren't there some who rob and steal all by themselves?"

"Only the smart ones," I replied.

I think Ez is right, sort of. If it had just been me or him alone, or even just the two of us, we wouldn't have turned into thieves. Maybe three or more people together is a dangerous number. That must be why they say two people can fight, but it takes at least three to create a riot.

Or a committee.

I was to learn soon enough that two people are enough to cause trouble, and I have to suppose that one can probably do it all by himself. What the hell are people all about, anyway?

Later, Ez and I picked a bucket of blueberries over on the Neck and left it at the Nichols' front door.

# {  CHAPTER 15  }

FROM BURIAL HILL, THE VIEW OF THE HARBOR SPREADS OUT: the old lighthouse over on the Neck; the sheltered waters between there and the town; the masts and hulls of the anchored vessels; the filled, bellying sails of those that are underway; all the rooftops stairstepping down the hillside to the waterfront; and the houses—mostly shingled or painted white, but also red, yellow, and blue—set along the winding streets. Because it's so steep, you can't really see what goes on at the docks from up there, just the tops of the masts and the roofs of wharfside businesses, not the cleaning and splitting of the cod that occupies several men at a time, all dressed in aprons, sleeves rolled, hats on their heads even under the roof. Nor can you see the cod drying racks on Skinner's Head, where row after row of fish turn into solid planks for sale all around the world.

The people who clean the fish are a funny bunch. They've got all kinds of odd ideas about their work, just like sailors do. The fellows out on the fishing boats believe stuff that can make you roll your eyes. Like if you get a hook in your finger, you should stick the hook in something—a rail or mast, maybe—because that will heal your finger quicker. Or some of the old guys wear rings in their ears because it's supposed to make you see better. Now, I ask you! And putting potatoes in your trouser pockets to keep from getting lumbago or rheumatism just doesn't make any sense at all.

The strangest thing the fish cleaners do is when they cut off a fish's head and pass the body on to the next man for splitting, the body wiggles as though the fish is still alive. The guy with the wiggling fish turns back to the one who cut off the head and has him smack the severed head with a mallet. I've only heard about this, but all the fishermen swear that it's true and that after the head has been hammered, the body lies straight. I guess it could happen, but I don't understand how.

I suppose if you spend half your life drifting around in a dory out there on the Banks, where the fog gets so thick you can almost eat it, and where if you get lost from your mother ship you may stay lost forever, and where your hands get cut by the lines you pull in out of water that's just above freezing, and where you do that day after day until you stiffen up like a dried halibut—well, I guess you might get some funny ideas about what works to make your life a bit more bearable, despite what tragedies might occur or what visions might appear.

Because she died only two years ago when the pneumonia plague, if that's what it was, swept along the coast and struck dozens of homes, I can remember my mother's face. Other faces have faded away. Good people died as well as bad people, and I can vouch that that's true. Not everyone who got sick died, but that only makes it seem more unfair. Sometimes everything seems unfair. First, my father, whose death forced my mother to sell our little house and move in with Grandpa Mike and Grandma, and then she went too, who was kind and loving, who helped me with schoolwork and sewed my clothes. Maybe she was like that other lady on the hill, too sweet for mortals here.

But, damn it! She wasn't too sweet, just sweet enough!

At some point while I was sleeping in the compartment, I saw both my mother and my father, and, again, I could make out only the wavy hair on the man, but the perfect picture of her. They were out in a little skiff under bluest skies with a steady light wind pushing them along, and both were laughing. But I wasn't with them.

I saw the gaff on the boat begin to bounce and from where I was—and where that was I'm not sure—I could hear it banging and thumping.

I opened my eyes, and the dream evaporated.

"Be quiet, you fool!"

I started at a rough voice coming from the after part of the boat. It must have been nearly dark out for the skylight hatch overhead showed only a hint of gray.

"What's the matter with you?" came a reply. "There's no-body to hear me."

"I don't care. We don't want anybody looking over here. Anything might get their attention."

By then, I was fully awake. I couldn't place the voices, but one of them was harsh and kind of scary sounding.

"Give me that pry bar and get out of the way."

Scraping sounds, then a sharp crack of breaking wood.

"Okay. Get below. We'll give it a few minutes before we get going. See if you can find the lamp, but don't light it yet. We'll have to go out in the dark."

I heard heavy boots coming down the ladder to the cabin, then muttering and shuffling, and the sound of something metallic being struck.

"Found it. Christ, I can't see anything down here."

"Never mind. As long as you know where it is. Come on deck. It'll be black in a few minutes and we'll shove off."

When I first heard the men, I assumed they were friends of Grandpa Mike's, but when the companionway hatch had been forced, I realized that they had no business being on the boat. No honest business, anyway. Now, it seemed that they were planning to take the boat away from the mooring, and that was something Mike would never have permitted.

What the hell was going on? And, more to the point, what was I going to do about it?

My first thought was to open the skylight and crawl out on the deck, but then I remembered that the hinge on the hatch needed oil, a job I had forgotten, and would screech like a scalded cat if I pushed it open. I tried to peer through the holes that had been bored in the door so that rope handles could be fixed on the other side, but even though I wiggled the knots on my side of the door, I couldn't see a thing. I could tell that it was dark in the cabin because the cracks around the door's edges showed no light. Overhead, the skylight was now dark as well. Night had settled on Marblehead.

As quietly as I could, I lay back on the sail, angry and now fully aware that I was trapped on the boat and that the two men who had broken in might not be overjoyed to find they had a witness. I had to get out. If I could just get ashore, I'd run to the harbormaster's house and tell him what was going on.

Still, there was that squeaky hinge on the skylight.

I rose as high as I could and spit at the hinge, maybe that would grease it enough to allow me to open the hatch without arousing the crooks who were still in the cockpit. Just try to spit quietly sometime. Ordinarily, I suppose, I could have spit all day, but now my mouth turned dry as a stove bottom. I tried to moisten the hinge, anyway. Cautiously, moving as slowly as possible, I slid back the barrel bolt that secured the skylight. I became aware that sweat was running down my sides, and I felt my eyes stinging. Gently, oh, so gently, I pushed on the bottom frame of the skylight and was terrified to hear the beginning rasp of the hinge. I froze, certain that I had given myself away.

After an agony of minutes, when the only sounds were those made by the boat and its rigging, I eased back down on the folded sail and attempted to cook up another plan. Unfortunately, none was in the oven. All I could think of was the two men in the cockpit who had broken open the companionway hatch and were planning to steal the boat. Something about the voices, particularly the first one, didn't make me think that they'd go easy on anyone who threatened to expose them.

"Okay," I said to myself. "There's got to be something I can do. It's dark. They can't see me. Of course, I can't see them, either, but I know the boat—and they don't."

Not that that would make much difference since the main cabin was nothing more than a cargo hold with a wood stove, a couple of water breakers, a cedar bucket, and hammocks tied against the hull. The rest of the space was taken up with storage bins running along each side, leaving only a small passageway between. With their lids down, the bins made good seats, and hammocks secured to the overhead could be unfolded and swung above them. Grandpa Mike kept common replacement parts on board—deadeyes, sheaves, blocks, and that sort of thing, along with a few bolts of canvas of varying weights, made-up oakum, and some small kegs of paint, pitch, and tar that were for sale, unlike the smaller cache of supplies in the forepeak locker that were used to maintain his own boat.

I never could figure out pitch and tar. You probably think any fool could tell the difference, and just about every fool has given it a try. Sometimes tar is made from pitch, and sometimes pitch is made from tar, and don't ask me to tell you how because I've listened to some of the old men along the docks arguing about weights, inches to a barrel, thickness, and a bunch of other stuff and a lot more about kettles, fire, pine knots, turpentine, and God knows what. From what I gather, one is thicker than the other. Unless it's thinner. There's even some tar made out of coal, but I don't even want to think about that.

But right then, I had other things on my mind. Maybe, I thought, I might be able to sneak into the cabin, hide in one of the bins, and make a dash for the deck when the men came below. Then I could dive over the side, grab onto the dory, and row like hell for the shore. But what if they had untied the dory? They must have come out to the *Mary Constance* in some boat of their own, but maybe they'd brought the oars onto the schooner, or maybe they never made their boat fast and had just let it float away.

As I chewed on these things, I heard the first man say, "Drop the bowline, Hump. The tide's turning. We'll let her drift off."

Hump? I'd never heard anybody around Marblehead called that. Was it short for something? Maybe it was a nickname for the way he looked. I was still in the dark, any way you want to take that.

Heavy footsteps sounded forward along the deck toward the skylight. Even though it was pitch black, I still feared that I might be seen. I ducked under the top fold of the sail and held my breath. Soon, I heard the steps retreating aft and became aware of a change in the motion of the boat. No longer was it rocking at the mooring, but was now floating free.

We were heading out, and I was caught as surely as if I'd been locked in jail.

Just then, I remembered the linseed oil in the forepeak locker. I could have brushed it on the hinge! Now, it was too late.

# { CHAPTER 16 }

MARBLEHEAD HARBOR SLANTS FROM SOUTHWEST TO northeast. It's long and not too wide, opening out into Salem Sound. Salem—that's where they killed those girls they said were witches, one of them from Marblehead, by the way—lies just to the north, while the Neck, almost an island, connected by a narrow strip to the mainland, makes the south shore of the harbor. The Neck, like the Marblehead shore, is about a mile long. It used to be one big farm, but now it has hotels and cottages and is a place where people go for picnics and such. There are no real problems inside the harbor, except for other boats, because while there are rocks close to the north shore, nobody but a fool or a daredevil would try to sail right up alongside unless there was a dock, like the one at old Tucker's Wharf. Oh, there are the Boden Rocks, all right, but they're far on the other side. And the harbor's deep with plenty of water under the keel all the way out to Salem Sound, but there you'd better start looking pretty keen, because all kinds of rocks and ledges are scattered around.

These guys, whoever they were, seemed to know something about what they were doing, but then everybody in Marblehead, well, nearly everybody, knows a little bit about boats and how to sail them. I once talked to a farm boy about sailing—he and his family had come by train for a visit to relatives in town—and I thought, at first, that I was talking to an idiot. He didn't know cheese about boats. I had to tell him that masts were the tall things that stick up from the deck, that booms are the long wooden poles that are parallel to the decks, and that the gaffs are the same, only a little shorter, and sit on top of the booms when the sails are furled. When the sails are set, the gaffs are raised high off the deck and hold up the four-sided sails for the wind to push.

As soon as he started telling me about farming, I realized that I was as dumb about that as he was about sailing and that, since I wasn't an idiot, he probably wasn't either.

I heard the foresail gaff being raised as the hoops slid up the foremast. They didn't make much noise because one of my jobs was to keep them greased. We heeled just a little bit as the wind caught the sail, and I could feel that it was coming from our port beam. I could tell when the peak was being tightened, just from the sounds. Not much was said, and what there was came from the rough-sounding man.

"Okay. Light the binnacle lamp so we can see where the hell we're going."

I heard the cap on the binnacle snap open and a match flared briefly, casting a slight glow that I could make out through the holes of the door handles.

"Stay on Nor'nor'east until I get a fix on where we are."

If they were going to Salem, they'd have to come over to a

northwest heading before long to get around Peaches Point, but if they were going to Boston or someplace at the south end of Massachusetts Bay, they'd have to swing to starboard and thread their way through the gap between Gordon Rock, at the end of the Neck, and Cat Island, or whatever they're calling it these days. People keep buying it and selling it, and every time some new owner comes along they change the name. I think the new guy, Pollard, he calls himself, wants it named "Pollard Island," but we were just getting used to it being named "Lowell Island," before that. Actually, most folks never pay any attention to these name changes and just keep calling it Cat.

It made no sense that they'd head for Salem. Everybody there knew Mike's boat, and what would be the point of sailing in there? Oh, they might want to strip it out, to piece out the cargo and the gear, but even at night somebody would probably notice and raise a rumpus. So I guessed that they were going to steer south pretty soon.

Since it was still high tide, even though it had begun to run out, they'd have plenty of water to make a run through, although, to be honest, if you know the approaches to Marblehead, high or low tide doesn't make that much difference. Once out into the open on a clear night, anybody would have been able to head down toward Boston Harbor, and they'd know about Marblehead Rock, for sure. I had made the run with Grandpa Mike several times, a couple of times in the dark, so I knew that the Boston Light would make the course obvious to an experienced sailor, and the big iron bell buoy should make it safe to go past the Graves Ledges. With daylight, they'd be able to thread past the islands, rocks, and other ledges. But, hell, once out in the Bay, they could be headed anywhere.

I felt the schooner changing course to port.

"Going to Salem, after all," I thought.

But I was wrong. They had merely headed her up to the wind, and now they were both heaving away on the main halyard and swaying the main up pretty fast.

The rough voice ordered, "Go tend to the jib," and there was clumping in the cockpit and forward on the deck.

Mike had rigged the boat for single-handing, snub-nosed, with only a stubby little bowsprit, about two feet long, hardly the rakish pole jutting out over the water that you see on most schooners. Bowsprits are nice to look at, thrusting forward of the stem and carrying sail the way they do, but we also call them "widowmakers" because a fellow trying to keep a perch on one of them in a pitching sea when one second he's plunged up to his ears in sea water, then kicked back up with canvas slapping his head and a loose sheet whipping him in the face, has a fair-to-even chance of falling off. He might be a wonderful husband, but he'd damned sure better be ready to ride the whirligig, or they'll be getting the hymn books ready back home.

The *Mary Constance* is what we call a "knockabout," maybe not as dashing to look at with no long sprit sticking out, but easier to handle. The masts are set a little farther aft than on most schooners as a result, providing more room on the foredeck, and that allowed Mike to set up a club-footed jib, a forward staysail with its own boom that tended to itself when you tacked or gybed. An iron bar, the horse, ran athwartships and made control of the jib a bit easier. Like the other sails, the jib had a downhaul running back to the cockpit so that whoever was at the helm could bring down the canvas without having to go up forward on the deck. You still had to go forward for some things, although not as often. It wasn't the way you'd rig a boat for speed, but when you worked alone, as Grandpa Mike did most of the time, it was a big help not having to worry about whether the jib was going to get hung up when you came about. That boom just swung across as easy as a garden gate, and the only worry was that you might be standing there when it did. If it didn't kill you, you'd probably be knocked over the side, and that would kill you. Lots of sailors hate a club-footed jib, saying they'd rather be slapped to death by a loose sail than batted over the side. I guess there's no really safe way to go to sea.

Mike also refused to use topsails on the *Mary Constance*, having found that he was able to get as much speed out of her as was necessary for the work he put her to, and that the lower rig was better going into the wind than those boats that flew everything but your grandmother's drawers up high.

That same heavy tread continued overhead as the man called Hump went forward to sweat the jib up in place, and then, after another pause as the boat put her nose to the wind, we fell off on the original heading. Now we were moving faster, and the noises of the sea multiplied. Anytime anybody tells you that sailing is quiet, just let it go. Unless they've heard the roar of the waves rushing by when a boat has a bone in its teeth, you'll never persuade them that being on a sailboat isn't like a Quaker meeting.

So they didn't turn. They didn't go to port and head for

Salem, and they didn't bear to starboard and make a run to Boston. They were going straight ahead, and I tried to picture what lay there.

For one thing, they still had Eagle Island, probably just off to port and pretty much dead ahead. Getting past that obstacle didn't get us out of danger, because there was a ten-foot spot to starboard just past Eagle, along with some unnamed rocks, and they'd come to the base of Cape Ann before long. Unless they were trying to go into Manchester in the dark, they'd have to make a sharp swing to the right to clear Bakers Island, and that might be a trick to pull off, although not as bad as it used to be before the new light was put in a couple of years ago.

Somebody finally figured out that too many ships and boats were crashing into rocks around here, and in the past few years most of the lighthouses have got those fancy lenses with the French names—Frennel, or something like that, except for down at Thacher Island where they still use the old reflectors, not the new lenses. The new ones cost a fortune, but the really big ones, maybe six feet across, can be seen for twenty miles or more. That makes all the expense and care—even dusting and polishing the lens every day, besides keeping the tanks filled with lard oil for the lamp—worth it.

Lamps seem to be simple things, don't they? Well, you just don't know. People have been tinkering around with lighthouse lamps for years, and they still have trouble with them. Take the oil. They used to use whale oil, but it's getting too expensive, even though New Bedford sends out hundreds of whalers to try to catch the sperm whales that give the best oil. Then they tried something called colza oil that's squeezed out of some kind of seeds, and you can bet that it would take a lot of seeds to supply all the lamps in the world and still have enough left over for lighthouses. And there's rock oil, but not very much of it, and seal oil, and that's even harder to get, and some of the Portugee who came from over around the Mediterranean stick to olive oil, but they bring it with them, and we don't grow any olives in Massachusetts. So for the past few years they've been burning lard oil, made from refined animal fat, and you'd think there'd be enough of that with all the cows, pigs, and sheep that are butchered every day. And there does seem to be a good supply, only a lot of it is pretty crude, smokes up any place it's being used, smells awful, and has some other problems as well. A bright fellow on one of the lighthouses figured out a way to keep it from turning solid in cold weather, so that solved one of them, but the other things have yet to be fixed.

Some settlers out west in Indiana found a way to mix turpentine with something else—alcohol, maybe—and were using it for lamps. They called it "camphene" or "burning fuel," and it worked just dandy until the lamps started exploding and burned down damned near half of Indiana. At least, that's what I've heard.

I was trying to calculate where we were, just guessing, because I couldn't see outside. From the slight angle of heel and the sound of the water running past the bow, I put our speed at no more than three knots, maybe less, and that meant that the wind was very light, but that wasn't a lot of help in giving me an idea of our position because I wasn't sure how much time had passed. Maybe an hour, maybe more. I just didn't know, and I was more confused because I didn't know how much time we had spent at the mooring after these guys had come on board. The best I could come up with was that we were not too far from Bakers, and, if that was so, we'd probably gybe over to a starboard tack before long.

And we did.

## { CHAPTER 17 }

IT COULD BE ANYPLACE. ONCE AROUND BAKERS, TAKING care to miss Great Misery and avoiding Gales Ledge, we'd be headed south, and there were endless possibilities, the way I saw it: we could pass Kettle Island, pick up Eastern Point and run into Gloucester, but people knew the *Mary Constance* there even better than they did in Salem. We could head down into Cape Cod Bay to Provincetown or, maybe, Plymouth. There were other towns scattered all around Cape Cod Bay but not much in the way of deep water going into them. Even Plymouth could be a nightmare, and, as for Duxbury, forget it. Another choice would be to keep going down over the Stellwagen Bank and out into the Atlantic. Christ Almighty! What was I into?

"Take the helm," the rough voice said, and I heard feet bumping as they apparently changed places in the cockpit.

"Now, where'd you find that lamp?"

"Just above your head, Sam. By your left hand, as soon as you get below."

The only Sam I knew of was an old, white-bearded codger who walked with one foot curled around a crutch and who couldn't have managed to swing up onto a deck if you had hoisted him with a parbuckle. So this Sam was a stranger, like Hump, and I didn't know who he was or what he looked like. Shortly afterward, footsteps came down the ladder into the cabin and, through the cracks around the door, I saw that the lamp had been lit. I wanted to see who Sam was, but I was so scared I was afraid I'd do some dumb thing and make a racket. If they were crazy enough to nick Grandpa Mike's boat right out of the harbor, they must be willing to face some pretty tough consequences. They also might not want me to be around. Like I said, I was scared.

In a little while, whoever was in the cabin went back on deck but left the lamp burning. Mike never did that. He said it made it harder to see in the darkness if you so much as looked into a light for a few minutes. The binnacle was different: it was kind of a rosy light, there, and that didn't bother your sight that much.

It seemed to be a good time to try something that had been knocking around at the back of my mind. If I could get the point of the marlinspike into one of the holes for the rope cabin-door handles, and mash down the fibers of the rope, I might be able to catch a peep at the thieves, and maybe even see something in the cabin that I had forgotten, something that might help me to escape. I had to do it slowly and quietly, though, because, with the lamp going, anybody who glanced down the companionway into the cabin just might notice a shiny metal point sticking out from the door. One thing in my favor was that the companionway was offset a couple of feet to port because the mainmast came down through the cabin directly amidships and the ladder had to be off to one side so that you could go up and down. Somebody would have to be right in front of the companionway in order to see all the way into the cabin.

All I needed was a little play, a little flattening of one of the rope handles, and with an eye right up against it, I should be able to see something. And, by God, it worked. I couldn't see much on the starboard side, but looking aft, I could take in everything to port. It was downright disappointing. I didn't see a blamed thing that would be of any help. But I didn't see either of the two men, and, at least for the moment, that was some relief.

I became aware of an easing of the boat's motion, almost as though we were dead in the water, although from time to time I could sense that a small puff of wind came along. This went on for quite a while, with both men swearing every now and then about the lack of a breeze. Then the sails started slatting, and that meant the wind had died completely. Gaff riggers set up a hell of racket in a calm if there's any wave action, at all. The gaffs, up high as they are, get tossed back and forth, and you can sheet in the sails as much as you want and they'll still bang from one side to the other. Even after you drop sails, the gaffs and booms always act like wild bulls trying to escape unless you tie them down, and that only works for the main if you have a gallows to rest the boom on. On the *Mary Constance*, the jib will drop down when you pull on the downhaul, and because it's club-footed, it acts like the foresail, heaving jerkily from side to side even though you tie it down. But these guys didn't lower the sails and just left them to smack one way and then the other. Damned hard on the rig, I thought, but as much as I knew Mike would have had a fit about it, there wasn't anything I could do.

So there we sat. Me jammed up forward, and the two crooks up in the cockpit. I couldn't believe it, and I'll bet they were wondering what they'd got into as well. They had sneaked the schooner right out of Marblehead without raising a yelp, and now they couldn't move. If we were still there in the morning, they stood a good chance of getting caught red-handed. Of course, if there was no wind in the morning, nobody else was likely to be moving either. But there's a funny thing about sailing: you can be running along with a fair breeze at your back, look over the water and maybe less than a mile away another boat will be becalmed. Maybe it would play that way and some other boat would be catching the wind while ours stayed put. Not much point in hoping one of the steamboats would notice anything. They never even looked at sailboats.

There was a situation a couple of winters ago, down by Martha's Vineyard, in the middle of a big storm, when a sailing ship—a pretty good-sized one—hit a ledge about a half-mile offshore and began to sink. The weather was awful, with lots of snow and a freezing wind, and the passengers and crew had to leave the deck and climb up into the rigging as the ship settled onto the ledge. There they stayed, praying that they'd be saved, and, sure enough, along came a steamboat, all lit up and her stacks smoking like Hell on a Saturday night. But did she stop? Of course not. Later, the captain said he'd seen the wreck, and even made out the shapes of the people in the rigging, but he figured they'd all be dead, so he kept on going.

It turned out that about half of them *were* dead, frozen fast to the spars and lines they had grabbed for their deliverance. The ones who survived were saved by some Menemsha people who put out fearlessly in small boats to rescue anybody who might still be alive.

I don't know what that tells us about steamboats, and Grandpa Mike always tells me not to judge everybody in a group from the actions of only one or a few, but I've seen enough of how steamships act around sailing vessels to know that their skippers don't give much of a damn for the whole lot of us.

Then it hit me! Grandma Ellen would have started looking for me! I had spent a couple of nights on the boat by myself in the harbor, but I had always told Mike and Grandma that's what I was going to do, and she'd know that I wouldn't stay all night unless I had taken plenty of food with me. As far as I knew, there was only some ship's biscuit aboard, and she'd know that I'd just as soon eat a pine plank. If you soaked one of those things for a while you might be able to choke it down, but there was no way that I'd give up her cooking for that.

I had another chance in that one old guy in town spends a lot of time up near the Fort so that he can see ships coming in or going out. He has a high-powered telescope, and he says he can see all the way out past Gloucester, I guess even to Cape Ann. And he swears that he can see people on Cape Cod on a clear day, but since he never lets anybody look through his telescope, we just take his word for it. The main problem is that he spends more time down in the town than he does up on the hill, and, because it's something he does for himself, nobody ever told him what hours to keep. Obviously, he spends more days than nights looking around, but in the summers, when the sun stays up as late as it does, he might be there until about nine. That usually means that he'll be late the next day, if he goes up there at all.

So my best bet would be on Grandma Ellen. But what could she do? She'd fuss around the house for a while, then go to the chandlery to make sure that I wasn't playing around there. She'd probably walk along Front Street and ask whether anyone had seen me. Eventually, she'd take a look at the mooring and discover that the boat was gone. That was a good thing because it would just be unthinkable that I'd take it by myself and go sailing off, particularly when bad weather was in the forecast. So, by now she should have got the harbormaster awake, and she'd have raised hell all over the docks asking if anybody had any idea about me and the *Mary Constance*. She'd also be waking the telegraph operator who lived near the train station, and she'd fire off a screamer to Grandpa's hotel. Not that he'd be able to get back to Marblehead before noon in any event. But that was all right.

For the first time, I felt a little better. As long as somebody was looking for me, I felt I had a chance of getting out of this mess.

# CHAPTER
# { 18 }

I STILL DIDN'T KNOW WHETHER THERE WAS ANY WAY TO get to shore. Were we towing the dory? Their boat? Both of them? It might make a big difference. If by some miracle I was able to get into the dory, I was sure I would be able to keep away from the schooner if they had no wind to sail on. But if both boats were hanging off the stern, they could get into one and catch me without much trouble. If the wind came up and they wanted to, they could probably run me down, and that would be that for Luke. Just then, as if to answer the question in my head, I heard Sam—hell, they could probably have heard him in Boston—giving it to Hump.

"You fumble-fingered son of a bitch! What the hell were you doing?

"I ain't no damned deck ape. I tied it on. I thought it would hold."

"Thought it would hold? You don't just think it's secure. You make damned sure! And now we're stuck on this barge whether we like it or not!"

So, now I knew. Both the dory and their boat, a skiff, apparently, were gone. My hope for an easy escape had departed with them.

Quite a bit of time passed, hours probably, and I wasn't feeling any better about my situation. That's when I began to think that maybe a steamboat engine might not be a bad thing. At least we'd get where we were going and I might be able to scamper off. I'd never say anything good about a steamboat when Grandpa Mike was around, but he wasn't here, and he might have changed his views, too, had he been stuck in that little compartment. But he'd have clunked their heads together hours ago and been done with it, and I can't. It sure takes a long time to get big.

Then, a slight feeling, like a big hand had pushed on the starboard side of the hull, and then another. In a moment, we were underway again, and we were once again picking up speed, but now the wind had shifted south and seemed to have more strength. We lay over slightly, and I heard the blocks running up topside as the sheets ran out. Well, there went my hopes that we'd stick in one place until morning.

Pretty soon we were jogging along smartly, the water singing on the planks outside my hiding place and the bow lifting and falling in a quick and easy motion. If I had been on deck, I would have loved it. This kind of sailing is what schooners are all about. Put a schooner on a reach with the wind rushing in from one side or the other, and there's not much on the water that can catch it. Down below, curled up under the flap of the storm sail wasn't anything I could say was a lot of fun, though.

I guess I could have been pleased to know that everything

I had stowed in the forepeak locker was going to stay where I put it, but nothing in there seemed to offer any hope. What was I supposed to do? Paint them into surrender? The *Mary Constance* was beginning to pound a bit by now, the rise and fall of the bow no longer a gentle motion, rather a quick thrust upward followed by a lurch down into the water. On deck that wouldn't get much notice, but down in the dark compartment, way forward where the movement was magnified, every time the bow plunged I wondered whether it was going to come back up. Of course, I knew it would, because she was a dandy boat, well-made and well-fastened, but I still felt uneasy each time I felt the bow start to fall and then heard the water rushing by above the level where I crouched on the sail, the schooner now laid well over on her port side. I got a little bit tired and I needed to take a pee, but there wasn't a chance that I could get out of the compartment and use the cedar bucket. I settled on using a half-filled jug in the locker that seemed to have turpentine in it. I'd have to remember that or Mike would skin me if I forgot to tell him and he tried to use it to thin some varnish. But I realized that unless something changed for the better I might not see him again and none of this would matter.

I was hungry, too, and even if I could gnaw through one of the biscuits, they were stowed aft by the stove, and I couldn't get to them. There wasn't anything to eat where I was hiding but some rope, and even if it was the best manila, and no knots in it, I'd have to pass.

Again, somebody banged down the ladder into the saloon, and this time I was ready to take a look.

A burly man in a loose, dark sweater and a cap of some

kind on his head was standing slightly to the right in front of me, back near the companionway. Although the lamplight was weak, I could see that a full, black beard covered most of his face, and his eyes—clear as cold, blue glass—seemed to be looking straight at me. I'd never seen him before. Some corner of my brain told me that he couldn't see my eyeball peering out that little opening on the rope handle, but the thought made me shiver anyway. He turned away, almost out of my range, and I could barely see him moving. He was bent over doing something, but I couldn't figure out what it was.

I got it: he was rustling some coal out of the bin, and then I heard him dump some of it in the belly of the stove. The stove was just out of sight, but I heard a lid clang, and pretty soon there was another metallic racket, and I guessed that he had put a pot on the top. Fiddles made it possible to use the stove underway. They're kind of like big clamps that hold pots and pans on the stovetop. Even though the boat is rolling, the fiddles grab the items loosely, allowing them to tilt but not slide off. You get an occasional splash or two, but they work pretty well. If the stove were smaller, you might be able to use gimbals, like on the lamp, which are little rings that swing athwartships and keep the lamp straight, the bottom moving first to one side and then the other, when the boat rolls back and forth. I've seen a couple of stoves that are gimbaled, but ours is just a big iron hulk that's bolted to the ribs and sole.

When the companionway hatch is open, smells go forward because that's the way the air usually moves on a boat. After a few minutes, I could tell that he was making coffee, and I'd have given anything for a cup. Not that I'm a coffee drinker, mind you, but anything hot and wet would have set well at that point. He didn't go back on deck but moved to stand with his back to me, hands resting on the ladder, looking up into the dark.

"What do you think we're doing now?" he shouted. It was Sam. That voice was unmistakable, a voice that cut through the other noises like a ripsaw.

"Must be five or six," Hump replied. "This wind seems to be building."

"That's all right. We'll keep on heading south for a while."

"I don't know if I can hold course much longer. She don't point very well and the wind's backing." Hump sounded a bit tense.

"I'll come up and see if we can bring her a point or two closer," Sam said and climbed back up the ladder. He carried two tin mugs of coffee, and how he managed to make it up topside, not spilling anything and without holding on to anything earned him high marks with me. I was hugging the foremast heel as hard as I could to keep from being tossed around in the compartment.

For the life of me, I couldn't produce a single idea that might make it possible for me to get away from this heaving, bouncing jail I was in. "Stone walls do not a prison make," somebody said, but if he'd been surrounded by oak and teak in the middle of a large body of water, he might have added, "wood does." Nobody was going to swim to shore, not even Hump with Sam on his back, a shore that I might not even be able to see. I had watched stars earlier, shooting up and down like rockets as the skylight rolled with the boat, but now I couldn't see anything bright, so I figured some clouds had moved in. The wind can come out of a clear sky as well as a cloudy one, although the way it had swung around from north to south or southwest and the fact that Hump said he wasn't sure he could hold her to the south made me think that those barometers back in Marblehead hadn't been wrong about dirty weather making up.

There was no place on deck where I might hide, at least not if anybody kept his eyes open. I could lie somewhere in front of the doghouse, perhaps, hang on to a mast or a shroud, and hope that nobody would see me. But that wasn't any better than where I was, which was certainly warmer and drier than up topside, and I couldn't get there, anyway. I'd always thought the Mary Constance was a pretty big boat, but it sure seemed awfully small now.

Loud voices from above got my attention. They were easing the sheets in order to let the Mary Constance fall off some, and the improvement in the boat's motion was noticeable. But it also meant that they had given up a point or two on their course because they now must be somewhat east of that. I was so confused about where we might be that I quit worrying about it, although the picture in my mind of the shape of the surrounding shores made me believe that whatever the thieves' plan had been, it was no longer working and that we were rapidly running out of chances to make much headway into Cape Cod Bay.

"Douse the fore!" Sam ordered, his voice clearly carrying down to me. Both men were yelling to be heard above the crashing sounds of the wind-driven waves.

It's a wonder I could hear anything with every piece of gear crashing around on the insides of the storage bins each time we pitched or rolled. Metal hit metal, metal hit wood, wood knocked against wood, and God knows what else was clanking, clattering, and bashing about.

We were taking some quick water over the bow, and I could hear it coursing down the deck as it ran down and off the side, like somebody was standing up there with a big bucket and splashing it all over at regular intervals. A really big bucket. That's when the drip started.

Now, I've said that the *Mary Constance* was a tight boat, and she was, probably as well-built and well-found as anything under sail. However, wood is wood, and planks are planks, and whether they are lapped or set edgewise one on the other, they move as a boat is driven through the water. Sure, you caulk the seams with oakum and then stuff pitch in to keep the water out so the fibers won't rot, but that's about as much as you can do. Sooner or later, the water wins a round. And you can seldom tell where the leak is. Because of the shape of a boat, the way the decks slant and the planks curve, water can work its way in at the bow and then cause a drip back aft. Usually, it's a deck leak that causes a drip inside, but don't count on it, especially when you are blasting along the way we were. The seams of the hull are underwater so much of the time, and the force of the boat slamming into the waves can push a surprising amount of water through a tiny opening. Then it drips inside. Of course.

I tried to move my head so that the drip missed me, but then the boat would roll and my head rolled with it and damned if the drops of water didn't seem to wait until I was directly under them before they let go and splashed down on me. I don't get too anxious when I'm in close spaces, but there in the dark, headed for who knew where, half-covered with the folded storm sail, I didn't want to cover my head, too. So I just went along with the dreary fact that not only was I tired and hungry, I was also getting wet. And I was going to get a lot wetter.

Hump the Clump, that's the way I was thinking about him, noisily made his was to the foremast after pulling the downhaul, and—the dumb sonofabitch—he was whistling! If there's one thing you learn early, it's that you don't whistle when the wind's already blowing unless you're toting an empty attic on your shoulders. Mike says it's okay to whistle if you've been becalmed for at least three hours, but not before then, and it's plain stupid to whistle up a wind when you've already got more of one than you can deal with. But I didn't hear anybody whistling while we were bounding up and down in the calm. So here was Hump warbling like a mockingbird right overhead while the gale tried to wipe the tune away before it got out.

If the wind was as strong on deck as it seemed to be, he was going to have a hell of time handing the sail because the canvas would be cracking back and forth and the gaff would be aiming to brain him as Sam brought her a bit into the wind. That little job can be vicious when the sheets get some slack and whip at your hands and face. Have somebody hit you as hard as they can with a piece of wet rope sometime, if you don't believe me.

We righted slightly, slammed hard into the waves a few times, and I heard the gaff on the foresail come banging down toward deck. The halyard and the topping lift took up the strain as the gaff bounced along on top of the foresail boom. Even though I was half-expecting it, it scared the hell out of me when it rattled and scraped back and forth until Hump got it secured. At least, I hoped he had secured it. After his work on the skiff painter, I couldn't be sure. Luckily, the spar hadn't broken loose and hit the skylight when it came down so I was still protected from everything except that miserable drip.

If I hadn't been so scared and feeling so all alone, I might have laughed at the two crooks: what a cock-up they had gotten themselves into. They had nipped the boat all right, sailed it into a dead calm, and now they had it in what was apparently a full gale. If they had thought they were in for an easy time of it when they came aboard in Marblehead, they sure had miscalculated. As I say, it was almost laughable. "Almost" is a word that can cover a lot of territory. I wasn't having an easy time of it, either.

If things didn't let up soon, they'd have to reef the main to keep her on her feet. And then...then I really started to worry. What if they decided to shorten sail some more and started looking around for a storm jib? If they found it, they'd find me, because I was wrapped in it with no place else to go.

Naturally, that's what they did.

# CHAPTER 19

"WHAT THE HELL IS THIS?" SAM HAD THE COMPARTMENT door open and stood before me with a look of utter astonishment.

I was petrified. If spitting had been hard, speaking was impossible.

He put out an arm and grabbed one of mine. In one motion he lifted me up and out into the cabin.

"Hump! We've got a stowaway!"

"We got a what?" Hump couldn't leave the wheel, but I could see his silhouette bent down as he tried to see into the cabin.

"What are you doing here, you little bastard?"

I wanted to cry, then, but I didn't. I just stared. He must have thought I was the village idiot, and he cuffed me once and shook me with both hands on my shoulders.

"I asked what you're doing here."

I babbled that I had been putting things straight in the forepeak locker, that I had fallen asleep, that I didn't know what was going on, that I wanted to go home, and where were we, and what was going on, and so on, and so on, until he slapped me again.

"Shut your gob!" he shouted in my face. "Who are you?"

I didn't know whether that meant I was supposed to talk or not. The last time I opened my mouth he told me to shut it. I ducked my head in case he tried to hit me again and blurted,

"I'm Luke."

"Luke, is it? Well, Lukey, you've made the biggest mistake of your life."

Sam pushed me up the ladder and out into the cockpit. He was really rough about it, and I fell to my hands and knees right in front of the wheel where Hump was wrestling to keep some kind of a course. I couldn't see much of Hump's face because he had a wool stocking cap pulled down low on his forehead and the collar of an oilskin jacket pulled up around his throat. I could see that he didn't have a beard, not a real beard like Sam's, but he surely needed a shave.

"Who the hell is that?" he bellowed.

"The owner's kid," Sam answered.

"No. He's my grandpa!"

Why I thought that was important, I can't say now, but somehow I felt I ought to set things straight.

"Toss him over, Sam."

Casually. Not a hint of a problem. Hump wanted me flung over the side without so much as a stutter. I just about died, right then. My chest felt like someone was shoving ice into it, and I didn't think I could breathe.

Sam's big boots were beside my head, and I cringed away from him as best I could. If he picked me up there was nothing I could do to keep him from giving me the old heave-ho overboard.

Just then, the boat caught a big wave, and the lurch made Sam sit heavily on the cockpit locker. Hump was swearing something fierce as he fought the wheel, and the boat surged off to port. I looked up at Sam who was staring at me with those hard eyes. Spray dripped from his beard and off the tip of his nose, which looked red in the small glow from the binnacle lamp. He was the scariest-looking man I'd ever seen.

"Come on, Sam," said Hump. "We gotta get rid of him."

Every time the boat pitched, more water rushed down decks, and some of it found its way onto the cockpit grating where I crouched. The air was full of spume from the waves, and I was getting soaked and beginning to shiver. I didn't want to die. I wanted to be home. I wanted Mike to save me. All of this was racing through my head at the same time, and in front of it all was the sense that there was nothing I could do.

Suddenly, Sam stood up, reached down and grabbed me around the waist with one arm, and I started to scream.

"Shut up or I'll feed you to the fish."

With that, he turned back to the companionway and shoved me below. Two tin mugs clattered behind me on the cabin sole.

"Pour us some coffee, and be damned quick about it."

I couldn't believe it, but I sure wasn't going to ask any questions. I was still on board, and I was still breathing air instead of water, and that's all I cared about. I picked up the mugs, filled them, and handed them one by one up to Sam, who passed the first one to Hump before taking the second for himself. He motioned for me to come topside, but I just climbed up two steps and stood there hanging on, half-up and half-down.

"You know, Hump," he said. "It ain't a bad thing having a cabin boy."

"Cabin boy's ass. He's nothing but trouble, and we've got enough of that already."

"That's why he's still here, you fool. It looks like we're going to need all the hands we can find if we're going to sail this witch through this weather."

As if to emphasize his point, the *Mary Constance* heaved up again on a big swell and careened like a sled on a mountainside before burying her port rail halfway up the deck.

"I can't hold her, Sam!" Hump cried. "We gotta fall off some more."

"Then do it. We'll let her go where she wants."

Sam let out the mainsheet some more so that we were now on a beam reach, just rocketing along through the angry water. I worried that the speed and the rolling might dig the main down into the water, but the two pirates didn't seem to notice. It was then I became aware that I could see some lighter areas off to the east, and I knew that we were sailing into a murky dawn. Ordinarily, the rising of the sun is a comfort when you're out at sea, but this didn't seem to be the kind of a day that you'd want to spend much time admiring. Gray waves, their white tops streaming spume and the breaking tops whisking downwind as they broke. In the distance it looked like the surface of an anvil that's been hammered for a hundred years, with horses' necks of white all the way to the dim horizon.

"My God!" Hump yelled. "That's a lighthouse!"

I poked my head all the way up through the hatch and looked to starboard with the other two. Barely visible, a long way off, was a flashing light, the new one that had been put on top of the twenty-five-foot stone tower just a couple of years ago. Race Point was at the very northern tip of Cape Cod's hook. And we were heading for it.

They had no choice now. They had to fall off, because it was clear they'd never be able to make it into Provincetown, and sure as hell we weren't going to make any more southing. As for the Point itself, there was nothing on that bleak shore that would be kind to a boat.

## { CHAPTER }
# { 20 }

I'VE HEARD THAT THEY USED TO HAVE BEACONS, SORT OF lighthouses, in the English forests so that travelers would have some fixed point that indicated where they were or where they were going. That wouldn't have worked in Massachusetts because the first thing the early settlers did was to cut down every damned tree they could see. They had to—or freeze to death.

Lighthouses exist so that sailors can see them from a distance and have some idea of their position. Most importantly, they tell you that you don't want to sail where they are. Some folks think lighthouses are romantic. Most sailors appreciate the fact that lighthouses tell them where the dangers are, but they really don't want to get close to them. Seeing one can give you a little lift of confidence in fixing your position, while, at the same time, you get a slight chill in the knowledge that the light is resting on someplace that can kill you. As Mike says, the ocean can be rough, but it's a featherbed compared to a rock.

We were hitting an incoming tide that curved around the

hook and pushed down into Cape Cod Bay, and it was met by the wind running straight at it, forming huge, short waves the way those conditions always do. Until you see it, you have no idea of the powers that meet and fight with each other in deep water. In some places, tides can run faster than boats can sail, even pushing them backward although, like us, they may have a strong breeze to sail on. The amount of water that flows in a swift tide must be like a moving liquid mountain. Now, put a thirty-knot wind blowing right against that river of sea water, wind that is already kicking up waves all by itself, and the collision pushes up waves that are hard to believe. But you believe them, all right.

"You, boy," Sam pointed at me. "Put on some slicks, get that storm jib up here, and we'll clap it on."

I was holding on for my life, and he wanted me to wrestle that rolled up sail up to the cockpit and then onto the foredeck! Well, I thought it was a crazy idea and was about to say so when he whacked me on the shoulder with a big, meaty hand and sent me sprawling over the cockpit coaming. I'd been hoping that he'd decide against trying to put the storm jib up, and I'd have agreed with him on that since I didn't think I'd be able to do it.

"When I tell you to do something, you move!"

I did. First, I tumbled below and pulled an old knee-length oilskin out of a cubbyhole on the port side. It would have been a little more than waist-length on a full-grown man, but it hung on me like a tent, with the sleeves falling down over my hands. I took a couple of rolls in the cuffs and crawled into the forward compartment to reclaim my former bed, only this time I wouldn't be lying on it unless I fell on my face. Which I did several times before I was able to clamber back topside with the heavy canvas sail.

Teak is what Mike had used for the decks and the cap rails. He'd had the wood brought in from someplace—South America or Siam or some faraway country—by one of the ships that came back from the Orient and rounded the Horn. Boston was full of things I'd call junk that people were buying just because it was unlike anything you could find in New England. Why folks think that pots covered with dragons and stuff they can't read is better than a plain piece of crockery is more than I can figure. But wood, that's a different matter, particularly when you need teak and lignum vitae and other special material to put into the building of a ship. The lignum vitae is for deadeyes and even in some blocks, while the teak is just the best thing for a deck. You don't varnish it, sand it, or oil it, and the sun and the salt water bleach it out to a whitish-gray which looks okay and has the advantage of acquiring little ridges where the softer part of the wood wears or washes away and leaves the raised, hard portion of the grain. It gives a great foothold. In cold weather, with water breaking across the decks, you have to wear boots, usually with felt socks, and sailors have been trying all sorts of things for years to keep from sliding and falling, sometimes with success—tying marline around the soles, for instance—and a lot of the time with failure, and so they fall down and get hurt. Bare feet work the best, but when there's ice on the deck, you've got to put something on. Rubber boots have finally got to the point where they work all right, and I don't know why Mike hasn't bought any. I guess he's not ready for everything new.

And ice isn't the only problem. Salt, when it's dried, can be as hard and grainy as sand, but you don't find much of that on a boat. The salt that comes aboard with the waves never really dries because the air is so damp, and you wind up with a kind of mushy stuff that actually feels greasy when you rub it between your fingers. And it's slick as gull shit if you step on it wrong. Fortunately, when there's lots of water coming aboard, it keeps the salt from building up by washing it back where it belongs.

Even though I was barefoot, I moved on all fours, sometimes pulling the forward edge of the sail with my teeth and grabbing onto shrouds and handholds as green water sluiced across the deck. I was up on the windward side—the high side since we were heeled over—and managed to avoid the deck sweepers that came gushing aboard. The oiled slick I was wearing was almost like a sail by itself, plastered to my body at one moment and blowing wide at the next. Twice I almost lost my grip, but I held on as hard as I could and finally, water soaking around my neck and down my chest, made it to the foremast. The first thing I did was to lash down the storm jib so it would still be aboard when I got ready to use it. I released the jib halyard and tugged crazily to free the jib sheet. As soon as I got it free of the cleat, it jerked right out of my hand as the wind whipped the sail to windward. Luckily, the sheet was long enough that the bitter end didn't fly all the way out. A hockle—a sort of a kink in its tail—caught on my fingers, and I was able to hold it. The sail was standing straight out, luffing like mad, threatening to flog itself to shreds and take my arm out of its socket in the process.

Quickly, I began the almost impossible job of pulling the boom back to the boat. Apparently, they were trying to head up, but each time the *Mary Constance* nosed to the wind, another wave knocked us back the other way. Nevertheless, I waited for the next try and tugged as hard as I could with every attempt, helped by the fact that the violent motion of the boat frequently spilled a little wind from the sail. After what seemed like a couple of days, I had the boom close enough in that I could cleat it off and start unlacing the jib. That job damned near broke my fingers. With one arm around the boom and the other pulling like a draft horse, I managed to get the canvas off so I could sit on it.

Next I had to secure the downed jib with a piece of line and begin the attempt at putting on the storm sail. I say "begin the attempt," because there was no way in hell that I was going to get the job done by myself. I yelled back for somebody to help me and after about ten of these bellows, Sam came lumbering along to give me a hand, looking like a soaked ape.

We finally rigged the smaller canvas but not without curses and yells and pinched fingers. Wet canvas under a strain is pretty close to being as malleable as a sheet of iron, and it took every bit of our endurance to beat the damned thing into place and fix the shackle that held the halyard to the tack. I don't know how Sam felt, but I was just played out, my hands numb, my eyes bleared with salt and stinging spray, and my teeth starting to clatter. I was panting like Bugle going after a stick and wanted to flop down right on the deck, but the up-and-down, corkscrew motion on the bow was no place for safety or comfort. Sam just kind of rolled his way from the bow back aft and seemed to fall into the cockpit. I slithered down the heaving deck toward him.

Just then, a rogue wave, a towering wall of black water, came roaring from aft, and we were pooped. I was already gripping tight on a couple of lines, but even so the onslaught of the water nearly carried me away. I blinked the sting out of my eyes expecting to see an empty cockpit. Not a chance. Sam had been knocked through the companionway hatch but had managed to grab the handholds on each side. He must have swung into the cabin and then back out. Hump looked like a weasel in a washtub. Water was still churning around his knees. His cap had been ripped off his head and was nowhere to be seen. The binnacle lamp reflected rosily off his bald head, and his eyes were wild. Sam was smiling.

"See, Hump. I told you we could use another hand. If we lose him, so what? In the meantime, we can keep her moving."

Well, she was moving, all right. All over the place. I thought again of people who say, "It must be so nice and peaceful on a sailboat." Right. But not where we were. The waves were in a fury, cresting in all directions at once. Sailors talk about "confused seas," and these were not just confused, they were downright out of their minds. I don't think I could have manned the helm, the way the rudder was pushing and shoving it one way and then the other. I give old Hump credit, there, although he was barely able to keep from being knocked over the side. I regarded him the way Sam seemed to regard me: better to have him on board to help, but if he went over the side, to hell with him.

"Go check the bilge," Sam yelled at me.

Again, I skipped below and pulled at the ring in the cabin

sole plank that covered the bilge well. Water was sloshing to the top.

"She's filled," I called up.

"Is there a pump down there?"

"A little one," I replied.

"Well, get back up here, and let's try the main pump."

The main bilge pump was worked inside the cockpit. A vertical iron rod, about four feet long, ran straight down to a pipe connected to the pump. At the top was a handle formed from the end of the rod where it had been hammered into a loop. Pulling up on the rod provided the intake stroke, and when you pushed down it discharged water out a through-hull just above the waterline. It worked fine when you could stand steady, both feet firmly planted, and push and pull without much trouble. Now, though, when you had to hold on to something solid to keep your footing, it was crazy. The only thing to hold on to was the pump rod, and Sam and I were both trying to lift up and plunge the rod down while we were hurled from side to side as the boat lurched. Another big wave hit us as we were firmly gripping the pump rod with both hands, and our combined weight suddenly thrown to the side bent the rod over like a wilted flower. We tried to bend it back straight, but all we managed to accomplish was to break the damned thing off right at the deck. We wouldn't be pumping any more in the cockpit.

"Okay. Turn on the other pump."

I skittered below, broke out the handle for the standby pump, and started to work. I don't know how much water each thrust of the pump put over the side, but it didn't seem to be making any difference. I pumped as fast as I could, and the water level in the bilge stayed the same.

"It isn't going down," I shouted.

"Keep at it."

So I did. I figured I ought to do what the sailors on the big ships do when they're working hard at something, so I started to sing:

> "Your money, young Jack, is no object to me.
> Pay the money down!
> Half a dollar's no great amount.
> Pay the money down!
> Money down, money down,
> Pay me the money down!"

I've heard them sing that one and a lot of others, and I guess I'm just not bright enough to know what they're singing about because I never have been able to understand any of their songs. They haul in the anchor singing "Bully, bully, bowline" or some other nonsense like:

> "We'll heave,
> Aye!
> And we'll swing,
> Aye!
> And we'll all drink brandy and gin!"

That one, I can figure out, but the fact is on a Yankee fishing boat they won't be drinking anything but coffee, tea, or water until the ship gets back in. That's what they say, although most of them carry a bottle in a boot. The British navy's straightforward with their grog ration, but Marble-head schooners get all holy about such stuff.

I pumped and sang and pumped and sang. Finally, I could see that the water had lowered by maybe an inch, so I went at it as hard as I could for about ten minutes, not even taking time to look in the bilge to see how I was doing. My arms and shoulders were aching, my singing had become a croak, and I guessed I had about run out all my scope. One more look and I saw that the bilge was now fairly clear.

"She's almost to the bottom," I yelled.

"Belay that and get back up here. You can check the bilge in a few minutes and see how much water we're taking on."

I couldn't have pumped anymore if my life depended on it—and it probably did.

# { CHAPTER 21 }

ON DECK, THINGS HADN'T IMPROVED, ALTHOUGH I COULD see that the Race Point light was now almost abeam, still a good way off to starboard. So we were making some headway, even though it seemed as if we were just sitting still getting pounded by the angry sea. There wasn't a prayer of coming about into the wind and trying to make a run back across to the mouth of Cape Cod Bay, and supposing we were able to do so, we'd never be able to make it into Province-town because the wind had backed some more and would be right on the nose when we tried to turn around the hook. Again, even if we could come about or wear ship so we could reach back across the Bay, what lay ahead? Ledges that run all along the coast from Scituate to Minot. Trying to work our way into Hingham would be virtually impossible and a mad act, besides. Should Sam decide to make for Boston, we'd be racing toward that mass of islands, scattered like buckshot, and not a safe harbor in the lot. In good weather with good visibility, such a run wouldn't be so bad, and an experienced navigator would be able to take fixes on Minot

Ledge light—if we still had a Minot light—and Boston Light and read the buoys so he could thread through the channels to Boston Harbor. Now, it would be foolhardy, and besides, for some reason, Sam and Hump obviously hadn't wanted to go to Boston in the first place and instead had shown themselves ready to face a furious ocean rather than go there.

And now the rain began. We'd had some fitful squalls before, but they skimmed by quickly and spattered us only briefly. Now, the upwind clouds opened up, and raindrops as big as a grapes came blasting horizontally across our deck. And they hurt. It was like getting peppered with birdshot. And the noise! Drums had nothing on the *Mary Constance*. The wind had been shrieking though the rigging for hours, but for some reason it now seemed to increase although the wind didn't feel much stronger. Does that make sense? A lot of odd stuff happens in a sea storm.

Sam, who had put on foul-weather gear earlier, and Hump and I in our oilies were bent over with our backs to the rain, and I guess we were all pretty miserable—wet and now getting cold. You can't keep water from getting down your collar or down your sleeves. You raise your arms up to haul on a line, and you feel water running to your armpits. And we had another problem. The way the boat was heeling, the end of the boom was getting awfully close to the water. It wouldn't be very pretty if it dipped down and filled the bottom half of the sail with sea water. It might split the sail or even take the boom off.

"The hell with this," Sam shouted and reached for the starboard main sheet.

He wrestled with it for a moment—the blocks had got a little twisted—and took a turn around a cleat before he began easing off. If he'd tried to hold the line without belaying it, that rough hemp would have burned through his hands like a saw blade as it ran out. We now had the foresail doused, the jib changed down to a handkerchief, and it was time to reduce the main, which was swung out wide. We were totally unbalanced for sailing, but luffing the big sail cut the sharp angle of heel.

Grandpa Mike always said that you reef a sail when you first think that it's possible that you might have to reef a sail. Don't dally about it, bring the damned thing in. But we hadn't done that and now we had a job on our hands.

"Lively, boy!" Sam yelled. "Help me with the main."

I popped up from the cockpit and bounced forward to the mainmast. Sam was right with me. The main couldn't be controlled from the cockpit, so we quickly set to letting the gaff off, easing the peak a little, till the big spar came sliding crazily downward, and, if it wasn't stopped, threatening to smash us overboard as it swept back and forth. When it was about two-thirds of the way down, Sam told me to belay, so we had canvas bunched in the lazy jacks but still tight and drawing at the boom.

"Haul in, Hump!" Sam roared, motioning for me to go help.

I danced back, my feet touching the deck only at odd instants as the boat moved up and down under me. Hump had started pulling on the sheet with its four-to-one purchase, but even with that kind of tackle power he was having a time getting the gaff in quickly. He grabbed the helm for an instant and brought her head up a point or two so we got some luffing. I tailed the line for him while Sam was trying to gain control of the bucking, slapping canvas.

When you reef, you should fold the sail neatly along the boom, lapping it from one side to the other. That's what you should do, and, when the weather's good and you have a full crew, you do it. Reefing on the *Mary Constance* in that blow was not exactly by the book. Sam grabbed at the sail-cloth, which immediately flopped out of his grasp, then he tried to embrace the billows of canvas, but even with the lazy jacks holding the bulk of the sail was unable to pull it in tight enough to tie in the reef points.

Of course, Grandpa Mike wouldn't have reefed that way. He'd have done it a lot sooner, but if he'd been caught off guard and the boat was really in trouble, he would more than likely have scandalized the main by dropping the peak down so that the gaff lowered at the aft end and caught less wind. That's kind of a last resort thing. Or, sometimes, it's easier to trice up the boom with the topping lift, sort of scandalizing in reverse, which not only reduces sail but also lifts it up out of the way so the helmsman is better able to see what's ahead, not that we could see much in that wind and rain. I hollered something about doing those things, but Sam ignored me. Either he couldn't hear in all the storm noise, or he paid me no attention. Not many grown-ups think a kid my age has brains enough to think up a headache.

Hump had wrestled the main in close to the rail, so I left him and jumped up to help Sam. Between the two of us— him throwing his arms around the downed sail and me ty-ing in the reef points—we got the sail secured. It looked like a lunatic's clothesline, with bulges and wrinkles and buckled edges, but it was tight.

"Head her up!" Sam shouted.

Hump did battle with the wheel again, and we nosed into the wind just enough for the jib to crack right over, back-winded. Then, with me helping, he eased out a little on the mainsheet so that we had an angle on the wind.

"Hold her! See how she does!"

Sam was keeping his head low in case we gybed the main and the boom came blazing across to decapitate him. I was crouching a lot lower than he was.

Now hove to, we slogged out of the mouth of Massachusetts Bay and bobbed slowly into the open sea.

"Tie her down, Hump."

The effect was immediate. Heaving to is one of the tricks of heavy weather sailing, and I'd only seen Grandpa Mike do it once, and that was just for a squall that blew itself out in about half an hour. The idea is to have the sails pulling in opposite directions—the jib on one side and the reefed main on the other. As the main pushed us upwind, the jib countered to move us down. I didn't think we'd done a very neat job of it, but we were definitely riding more easily. What we had was two forces canceling each other out, and the boat was moving slowly forward and drifting downwind at the same time.

It's a funny thing how a sideways drift flattens out the water a little bit. Of course, you have the waves hitting the hull, but the way we were easing forward took some of the steam out of them, and then the movement of the hull downwind was like a big hand brushing across the surface so that as it moved it left a flatter piece of water behind. Not much, I'm here to tell you, but anything was better than what we'd been taking before that. Some of the skippers carry oil jugs, which they empty into loose-woven bags and hang over the upwind side. Apparently, this also flattens out the water somewhat, although I never saw any of that stuff on the *Mary Constance*. There was that linseed oil in the forepeak locker, but I was damned if I was going to volunteer to crawl up there to get it.

Rain sometimes flattens a sea, but that's only when you get a downpour with very little wind. Maybe the pelting we'd been getting had some effect on keeping the waves from breaking as much, although the force of the wind was so strong that even a cloudburst wouldn't have made much difference.

Sam told us to get below. Hump and I clambered down to the cabin and were surprised to find that things were a lot more comfortable there. This was the first time I'd had to look at the men who had shanghaied me, and I took the opportunity to examine them.

Hump may have been a handsomer fellow on shore, but he had been at the wheel for several hours with only a few breaks when Sam took over, and he looked thoroughly worked over, thin, wiry, and bushed. Without his cap he seemed less threatening, although his features were still fixed in a bitter mask. He fished a piece of flannel out of some recess in his clothing and wiped it across his dome as water streamed down his pinched face. His crazy eyes still had life, though, and they bored into me the way a moray eel looks at something swimming by.

All at once I realized that I wasn't scared any more. Some-where in the rain, the work, the noise, and the god-awful motion of the boat, I had become calm. It wasn't so much that I was feeling brave as it was that I simply accepted my situation and decided that I'd better do what I could to help keep us afloat and intact. I couldn't get away from the pi-rates—for that's what I now thought them to be—and it was pretty obvious that they needed me as long as the storm persisted. What happened after that was not only so far in the future that I couldn't picture it, but I also didn't give a great damn. There wasn't any future, anyway. Just the need to survive the present.

# { CHAPTER 22 }

"Okay, boys," Sam said. "We've passed the Point and we're hove to. Now this damned storm can't go on forever, but even if it does, we've got to be ready for it."

"I don't like it, Sam. This thing has backed so far, it's going to be turning into a regular nor'easter, and we've got nothing but lee shore for fifty miles."

"So, what do you suggest, Hump?"

"Well, maybe we oughta just cut out of this mess and run down toward Boston before it gets too bad. We can tuck in behind one of the islands and ride it out."

"That's your suggestion? Well, I don't plan to go howling down the Bay with rocks scattered like the Devil's marbles. We'd tear the bottom out before we went five miles. Hell, we can't see the light on the Point any more."

I sat silent. They debated for a few more minutes, but it was foregone that Sam was the boss and that Hump was going to play it his way.

Sam turned to me. "What were you yelling up there?"

"When?" I put on my innocent face.

"When we were rassling that damned main down."

I wasn't about to say anything about tricing or scandalizing or anything else that might set him off.

"I was just saying that it was pretty tough."

"Yeah? I thought you were trying to say something important."

"Not me," I lied.

I have to admit that I was feeling pretty smug. I knew about things that these guys didn't, about reefing early, about tricing and scandalizing, and that meant that they weren't as familiar with sailing a schooner as I'd thought they were. I suppose that should have made me more fearful because, after all, they were in charge and what they did with the boat affected me, too. Still, as old Thackeray said, more or less, "All is Vanity," and my vanity was that even if I was the captive of two pirates, I might be smart enough to get out of this mess alive.

Maybe that wasn't Thackeray. It might be the Bible. I'm not sure. One thing I was sure about: they weren't as good as a Marblehead schoonerman.

"Well," said Sam, "looks like we're in for a little longer ride than we planned on, right?"

He was looking at Hump who had parked himself on top of one of the bins. I think it held marline and beeswax.

Hump just stared down at the cabin sole and kept wiping his damned head. Either he was trying to polish it, or he'd forgotten what he was doing.

Sam told me to pour him some more coffee, and I did, putting a bit in another cup for myself. I've never figured out how you can get soaked to the skin, water in your ears and everything and still be thirsty. And I was. I gulped down the black stuff like it was sarsaparilla.

Sam fixed me with those frozen eyes.

"You gave me a turn," he said. "I think I must have jumped a foot when I opened that door. Thought we had a ghost or something on board. Now, tell me again, what the hell were you doing there?"

His voice still had that hard edge to it, although it wasn't so bad now that he didn't have to yell to be heard.

Just after he caught me, I had babbled, making no sense. So I told him again, this time with more connections in my thoughts. I explained that I had been doing some work for my Grandpa and that I'd fallen asleep after I finished.

"And your Grandpa. What's he do?"

"He's a chandler," I answered. "He has a store in Marblehead, and he delivers things to ships that need stuff but don't have time to come over and pick it up themselves."

"So this is a floating shop, is it? Well, that's worth something. Let me tell you sonny, Hump and I have had it pretty hard for the past year or so. When we were your age we both worked a bit around the docks, then we got into the mills and tried to make good lives for ourselves. But then we lost our jobs down at Fall River. Been out of work ever since. Had some trouble in Boston when we went there and got ourselves in jail, and we don't plan to go back. I thought I'd better let you know that we're not just a couple of stiffs who took this boat for the fun of it. We need a new start, and this is it. Don't get any funny ideas."

I nodded with all the enthusiasm of somebody who didn't have a single idea, funny or otherwise.

Hump rousted himself enough to give me one of his nutty glares.

"Don't forget it for a minute. We intend to take care of ourselves, and no snotty-nosed kid is going to get in the way. One wrong step and you're over the side. I think that'd be the best thing anyway, but Sam figures you might be some help."

I'd already been "some help," and I didn't see how I could do much more. I was totally in their control—they were both full-grown men and appeared to be healthy enough. One swat and they could put me down in the deep, and that's one place I never wanted to go. Grandpa Mike always said that a boat was meant to float and that if the boat ever got in trouble, stay with it and don't do any monkey tricks thinking you were bigger than the ocean.

"Pardon me, sir," I said to Sam. "But could you tell me where are you bound for?"

Sam put his head back and barked out a laugh.

"Shit, sonny. We don't have any more idea than you do," he finally choked out.

"We're stuck on this scow, headed for Europe, for all we know, in the middle of a goddamned storm, and we don't have a notion about going anywhere for certain."

"But we've got to go somewhere," I said nervously. "We've got to have some kind of a plan, some kind of a course to set."

"Right now, we've got to keep this bucket on top of the water. That's all we can do, if we can do that. If the weather lets up a little, then we can set the sails and make for some port or other. But at the moment, we're just rocking with the waves, and with a little luck, we'll keep on doing it."

It didn't make much sense to me. I understood that hove to we weren't going to make any course except the one the wind chose for us, but it seemed to me that we should have at least some tiny idea of what we were going to do once the storm let up enough to let us go back topside. God Almighty! I just then realized that I was thinking "we," as if I were part of the operation. "What we were going to do!" That was crazy. "They" were going to decide what I did, and I didn't figure to have any say in it.

# { CHAPTER 23 }

"Mr. Sam, sir," I said. "How's my grandpa going to make a living without his boat?"

"I don't give a rolling goddamn how he makes a living. He doesn't care about my living, so why should I care about his?"

Sam's face had hardened again, and I knew that there was a line I had to be careful not to cross.

"Your grandpa seems to live pretty well if he's got a boat like this and a store, to boot. Hump and I don't have anything but the clothes on our backs, and you can see that we're not likely to be invited into a Beacon Street parlor dressed as we are. Now, we've got this boat—or maybe it's got us, I can't tell at the moment—and, when we get a chance, we'll turn it into something for ourselves."

Hump finally stopped shining the top of his head and offered a "Damn right."

He certainly didn't appear to be the smartest character among us, although he had shown that he was fairly capable by the way he had fought with that wheel for unbroken hours, and he had clearly indicated that I was something he'd jettison without batting one of his beady eyes. I couldn't understand how these two had hooked up together, one loud, tough, and, under the right circumstances, probably a pretty gregarious sort, and the other an intense, withdrawn outcast who most likely kicked cats and slapped women. At least, that's the way I was seeing them at the time.

"The kid's right about making plans, Hump."

Sam had wedged himself securely between the butt of the mast and the aft end of one of the bins.

"Right now, we're probably four or five miles off the Cape, tending just a shade south, so if this wind keeps on going back we'll have to follow it up, try to wear ship, and make for Nantucket or someplace down there."

"Why go there?" Hump asked. "That's a bad place to get into. You've got shoals all over the place down there, I've heard. And we don't know the ground."

Sam turned to me.

"Where's your old granddaddy keep his charts? He must have some."

I reached back into a cubbyhole between the ladder steps to a long black box and pulled it out. The fastenings were leather tabs that had small slits cut into them, and these were pushed down over round-headed nails that stuck out for about an eighth of an inch. I flipped them off and opened the lid. Inside were carefully folded charts marked with lots of dots and lines that had been drawn onto the surface by Grandpa Mike's hand. It gave me a turn to see them, and I wished he was here to tell me what to do.

Mike had fashioned a table that slid up and down on the mainmast where it ran through the cabin. When the table wasn't in use, it was pushed up to the overhead and held in place by a wooden pin. It had a folding leg that was also secured by the same pin, and, when the pin was taken out, you could let it slide down to where the unfolded leg would sit in a slot and support it on the cabin sole. I showed Sam how it worked, and he brought it down and unfolded some charts on the surface.

"Let's see. We've got Boston Harbor, Gloucester, Cape Cod Bay, and—here we go!—this is the big chart of the whole damned area. Lookee here, Hump. We must be about here." He pointed to a spot east of Race Point. "Now, we move on down the coast and, well, shit, there's nothing till we get to Chatham, and it doesn't look too hot to me."

"My God," said Hump. "Nothing but sandbars and beaches."

"That's it, all right." Sam frowned and studied the chart some more.

"We can probably get into Chatham if the tide's right and we don't have too much wind, but I think Nantucket, even if it's dodgy, would be a better place to go. See, there's a marker here outside this place called Pollock Rip, and a couple of others on down the channel."

I guess I didn't expect that buoys would be so far down the coast, which shows how little I knew about navigation. Grandpa Mike had told me about how the government was trying to get bigger and better buoys outside harbors and along the major entrances. He said until a few years ago, the navigation markers were just a hodgepodge of sizes, a lot of them just floating spars of all shapes and colors, and were just as likely to put you aground as warn you off. Now, since the government down in Washington had finally awakened to the fact that the new steamships were going to get bigger and faster, they'd better do something before one of them ran onto Beacon Street in a fog.

That's why we have red and black buoys around Massachusetts and Cape Cod Bays. The red ones are always on the right when you are going toward the harbor and always on the left coming out. Same with the black ones: on the left going in, on the right coming out. There's a little saying "red right, returning" that's supposed to keep this in mind, although if anybody is so dumb he can't remember red is on the right he shouldn't be on the water anyway.

Of course, just because Grandpa Mike's chart showed that there was a marker at Pollock Rip didn't mean we'd see it, even if we got there, which was a long shot from being a sure thing. Sometimes, the buoys got washed away in storms or dragged away from the reef or shoal they were supposed to indicate, or they got pulled under by a strong tide if the water level rose and the chain that held them was too short. Add to that the fact that a bobbing marker, hidden behind high waves in poor visibility, can be impossible to locate.

And knowing where you are in relation to where the marker is supposed to be is another chancy matter. A boat that's caught in a strong crosscurrent can be pointed right at a buoy, and you might think that's all you need to do, but unless you keep an eye out on where it's going sideways, you can get in a mess of trouble. If you have high bluffs or prominent landmarks of any other kind, you can sight on them, and if they're printed on the chart, you can get a fix on your position by crossing the angles you get from your sights. But if you're talking Cape Cod, you've got problems. It's one long stretch of sand with some bluffs up at the north end, then beaches and dunes, each one looking pretty much like the other, marching along down the coast, backed by some unremarkable wooded hills farther back. I suppose on a clear day Mike would have been able to identify particular trees back inland or little shacks that might be situated along the way, but for people who depended on the chart to tell where they were and who didn't have much experience with one, that stretch of endless beaches printed on the chart didn't offer much help. And, not to put too fine a point on it, visibility in the storm was just plain shitty.

But, as I say, we weren't anywhere near Pollock Rip. We were, at Sam's best guess, way up east of Race Point, drifting in a storm that showed no signs of dying off, and with the very good possibility that it was going to keep on going counter-clockwise until it shoved us back toward the beach. We should have some running room by now, having been hove to for quite a while. The day had never brightened much, and thick clouds scudded across the sky almost indistinguishable from the inky waves beneath.

"Hump, you'd better get some sleep, and you too, Sonny."

Sam must have been as tuckered as Hump and I, but he knew we needed somebody to stay awake in case things got worse. I wasn't about to argue with him, and Hump didn't say a word, just reached up and pulled the hammock off the port side, fixed it on the overhead hooks and clambered in, boots and all. Sam was sitting under the other hammock and didn't appear to be ready to move out of the way so I eased my way forward and piled up on the coiled anchor rode, wishing I had the storm jib again. Nearly a full day of this, and I was right back where I started.

## { CHAPTER 24 }

"OKAY, HUMP," I HEARD SAM SAY.

I had no idea how long I'd been asleep, but it couldn't have been more than a couple of hours. I could hear Hump groaning as he rolled out onto the top of the bin he'd sat on earlier. I hoped they'd leave me alone for a while. But that wasn't in the plan.

"You there, Luke!" Sam, back to his rough-edged voice. "Hit the deck and get back here!"

I was stiff and sore, and my eyes were almost stuck shut, but I had to do what I was told. By now, I was sick of the whole thing and almost didn't care what happened to me. My stomach was trying to digest itself and my bladder was hurting. Nothing for it but to waddle down between the storage bins and see what torments awaited me.

"Is there anything to eat on this scow?"

"There should be some pilot biscuits somewhere."

I dug around in a little locker high up on the port side and found a square tin box, about a foot each way, and brought it out. Inside were stacks of white tiles that were masquerading as something edible. I passed them around and we set to work. Teeth were of no use so we soaked the miserable biscuits in our cups of coffee, but they were impervious to the liquid. I took a hammer from a toolbox, and we put our sorry fare onto the cabin sole and pounded until we had a small pile of crumbs that we distributed and poured back into the cups. That did the trick. Coffee mush. We repeated the process several times and reduced the supply of biscuits down to a handful, and by that time we'd had about all the coffee and all the crumbs we could stomach. Even so, it was good to feel there was something other than wind in our guts.

Hump was moaning about losing his cap. He said the damned rain was coming down so hard that it hurt the top of his head. I guess that would be true. I'd never thought about what it would feel like to have those big drops pounding on a bare scalp, and I said maybe there was shawl or something in the ladies' bin that he could put on his head. When we looked in the bin, all we could find was some lace trim, some whalebone stays, several rolls of different colored ribbon, and a couple of sunbonnets. Hump pulled them out and tried one on. It was way too small. The second one, a blue-patterned thing, fit, and he tied it under his chin. Sam snorted but didn't really laugh, and I ducked my head to wriggle back into my oilies so I could snicker without being noticed. Lord, but old Hump looked like a flower in an outhouse.

When we opened the hatch to the encompassing gray daylight, the noise was like an orchestra of lunatics, every piece of rigging playing a different, screaming tune, the notes sounding from low to high. Sam stayed below to make another fruitless search of the chart, and Hump led the way as I hauled myself up the ladder behind him, back to the cockpit—what we were supposed to do there escaped me—and gazed around at the towering waves with their graybeards streaming off downwind. About a half-dozen stormy petrels were floating on the water as if nothing much was going on. Those birds can ride out anything, I guess. They only take flight if a wave top comes breaking down toward them, and then they only scamper a short distance before taking the same positions they had before. It's really strange because there they are little bits of feathers, meat, and bone, and they can ride better than the best boats that any man can design or build.

Hump examined the lashing to make sure that it hadn't chafed and that the helm was still held firmly in place. I couldn't see that there was much I could do, but I checked the running backstay, then looked around to see if there was any land or maybe even another vessel in sight. There wasn't. We were still alone, even though I knew that there were probably some other boats that were caught out in the storm and were trying to beat back into the Bay and find shelter somewhere. The chances of running into another boat in the ocean are slight; however, no matter how long the odds, it still happens.

I tried to keep from looking at Hump in that silly bonnet, but I couldn't avoid it. He caught me staring at him, and I had to say something just to keep him from getting riled.

"Where are you from, Hump?"

"Goddamn it, don't call me Hump. Sam's the only person who can get away with that."

"I'm sorry. I didn't know. What is your name?"

"It's Humphries. Percy Humphries."

I was stunned. Standing there, soaking in the rain, a stupid, dripping sunbonnet on his head, was the heartless sonofabitch who wanted to drown me, and his name was—Percy! I started to blare out a laugh, caught myself, and jumped up on the doghouse with a whinnying cry that I was going forward to look after the jib. I'd be surprised if he understood anything I said because I was laughing and choking and trying to get out the words at the same time. Percy! For God's sake.

I took my time crawling back from the bow. Of course, there was nothing to see there, anyway, although I really did examine the lines holding the jib and the foresail. Chafe is more of a problem than you'd imagine. Every line that's in use on a boat is in danger of wearing through, and you have to look closely all the time or one of them will be silently rubbing against something else with every movement the boat makes, and they're stretching and relaxing all the time. Sometimes, it takes weeks for chafe to work its damage, but there are other times when you can put on a new run of manila, and, if there's a lot of up and down, back and forth movement, the strands will wear through in minutes. Somebody figured out that a line might rub several thousand times a day, so you understand the problem.

By the time I got done up forward and had worked my way back to the cockpit, I was so miserably wet and cold again that even the outlandish sight of Hump, excuse me, Percy, was no longer cause for merriment. We locked ourselves in place, feet hard against the bulwarks and our hands gripped around anything that was available, and rocked, lurched, rolled, and twisted for what seemed to be endless hours. We were beginning to lose what little daylight we had.

Sam banged the hatch open and poked his head out. He looked like hell, but I guess we all did. His eyes registered the fact that we were no better off than we had been and that the storm hadn't given up an inch. It was hard to tell which way we were headed or where we'd wash up. There didn't seem to be much we could do, but Sam thought there was something.

"Luke, haul your ass down to the forepeak and bring out that anchor rode—not the anchor, just the rode."

I didn't bother to ask why because I knew what was coming. We were going to stream a warp of the anchor rode over the stern as a sea anchor to slow our progress. I don't know why Sam didn't get the rode himself, since he was a lot bigger and stronger than I was. Maybe the biscuits didn't agree with him.

I worked my way through the cabin and into my former sleeping quarters and started working to get the rode free from the shackle which attached it to the anchor, all the while being rolled from side to side in that cramped area. Eventually, I worked it loose and then began the chore of dragging the heavy rope back through the cabin. It wasn't coiled, of course. You can't really coil that thick stuff, and it's faked down in a kind of figure eight. I'd tied some small stuff from the forepeak locker around a couple of bights in the rode so that it would stay in one bundle as I wrestled it aft. At least Sam helped me get it on deck.

Putting the rode over the stern wasn't easy. We had to secure one end to a cleat on one side of the stern, then unroll the rode so that it would run free when we put it over the side, but we had to secure the other end to an opposite cleat in order for the whole thing to make a big loop in the water. The rode was about three hundred feet long, thick, and had developed hockles that made it difficult to get straight. We finally got it over the stern, and when we felt the drag we knew that it was slowing us some.

Hump, squinting from the rain drilling his face, seemed intent on something in the gathering dark.

"There's a light, by God!"

And so it was. We looked at each other, nobody sure what we were seeing, just a pinpoint of light that came and went fitfully way off to starboard. How far off we couldn't tell. Sam jumped down the companionway, feet never touching the ladder, and hauled the chart back to the table. He brooded over it, muttering to himself, and then came back on deck and announced that he figured it was the Highland Light, on the Cape, one of the highest lights around because it was built on a bluff on the eastern side of the peninsula.

Well, that helped some. We still didn't have much of a fix on our position, although by looking across the compass at the light, we could at least get a line of position, even though we didn't have a notion as to how far off we were. I knew that Mike kept a book, a ledger of sorts, that he wrote things in that helped him navigate the waters around Massachusetts Bay and the Cape. I told Sam that I'd like to take a look to see if it might be helpful to us, and he nodded for me to go ahead.

I found the book and read quickly through the pages of

Mike's clear handwriting: shoals, shifting channels, missing buoys—all kinds of information about the waters he sailed. And then, hallelujah! A list of lighthouses and their characteristics: how high they were; were they white, red, or black; whether they were towers or block buildings; and their range. Highland Light, because of its height, should be able to be seen at a distance of twenty-five miles. Well, on a clear night on a smooth sea, maybe, but in the weather we were in that was probably a lot less, but at least we knew we were within that twenty-five-mile range. And it wasn't close, that we could tell. So, we guessed that we were maybe fifteen miles out, or perhaps a bit less. Why that was comforting knowledge, I can't say, but it sure lifted my spirits, and I think the others felt the same way.

I guess there are times when the sea just likes to piss people off because we had no more than taken a brief moment of satisfaction in knowing vaguely where we were when it all went to hell.

# {CHAPTER 25}

A LOUD CRACK, LIKE A WHIPLASH, SOUNDED OVERHEAD. We all looked up, at first seeing nothing. Then I noticed a line or a shroud swinging straight out in the wind, right up by the cap of the mainmast. The others saw me pointing, and they too watched silently, trying to absorb what we were seeing.

"It's the damned spring stay," Sam roared.

And he was right. The spring is the stay that runs between the top of the foremast and the top of the mainmast, a stout piece of cable, thick and taut. All of the stays are sort of connected by their function, and, to be really simple about it, that's to keep the masts up. Not that they're going to fall over unless something really pushes them. The forestay goes from the bow to the top of the foremast and keeps it from falling backward; the backstays run from the stern to the top of the mainmast to keep it from falling forward. On most schooners, like the *Mary Constance*, there are two backstays, one on each side, running backstays, or runners. When the boom swings out to one side, the stay is freed there while the second stay is secured on the other. Otherwise, the boom is so long that it would slam into the stay and maybe bring down the mainmast. Of course, the way things are all tied together, if you knock down one mast, you might also snap off the second one as well. In between the mainmast and the foremast, the spring stay takes up the strain that pulls the foremast back while at the same time pulling the mainmast forward. It's like a ring of tensions that holds the masts in place fore and aft. The shrouds do the same thing on the sides of the masts, holding them up laterally. And now we had nothing to keep the two masts from bearing too much fore and aft strain.

You look at those big spruce spars—the two masts—on a schooner like the Mary Constance, and you think they are so strong they can stand anything. You'd be forgetting that without the shrouds and stays, they'd be whipping about every time the boat heaved or rolled. True, the wood can take a lot of pressure one way or another because it's flexible and the masts are stepped through the deck and all the way down and butted onto the keel, but it's that back and forth and side to side movement up high that gets you into trouble if there's nothing to support them.

"We'd better douse all sail," I yelled.

And for the first time, both Sam and Hump agreed with me. With the spring stay gone, the strain even our reefed-down sails would put on the masts was too much. I didn't even consider fiddling with the downhaul in this wind but scampered forward and let go the jib halyard, pulling in on the jib sheet at the same time and trying to keep the sail from dropping into the water and filling. It dipped a couple of times, but it had spilled the wind, so I was able to get it back on the foredeck where I quickly squashed it down on the deck until I could take a couple of wraps with a piece of line and then tie it down.

Aft, Sam and Hump had finished dropping the main gaff and tamping down the little bit of sail we had left up after we had reefed.Together, we fixed the other running backstay so that there would be equal strain, and Sam and I released the spare main halyard and led it to the base of the foremast so that there would be a little bit of support fore-and-aft for the mainmast. Now, we had no sails at all, just bare poles. A major point about sailboats is that if they don't have sails, you can't sail them. Not only that, but we had now lost the easy motion of heaving to and were simply lying a-hull, letting the wind and water play with us as they wanted. What they wanted was to throw us around like butter flecks in a churn, but the hull offered enough resistance to the wind that we were able to push her nose away from the direction of the gale and move with the wind.

The three of us stood silently in the cockpit, each holding onto something solid for support. I had an idea what was coming, and I had lowered my head just as if I expected a blow. I got what I thought.

"Somebody's got to go up there and fix that stay," Sam said.

"It ain't gonna be me," said Hump without so much as a pause.

They both looked at me, and I didn't even bother to protest. I had figured that one out before they got around to it. I was the smallest and lightest, also the youngest and most agile. What they didn't know was that I was the one who had put the spring stay on in the first place and knew how to rig it, although when I put it up there we were moored safe and quiet in Marblehead and the masts barely moved. Grandpa Mike figured I needed the experience of working high off the deck. Well, that's what he said. I was almost glad that he wasn't there so I wouldn't have to explain why the stay carried away, but he'd have understood that in the conditions we were in, with waves bashing us and the wind pummeling us, some things break even if they're rigged right. I wished with all my might that he was there.

But I also wished right then for something else.

"Mr. Sam," I said plainly, "I'm not going up there without a knife."

"What do you need with a knife?"

"I don't know, but I sure as hell don't want to have to come all the way back down to get one if I find that I need it."

You could tell that Hump didn't care for that idea, but Sam simply pulled his own knife off his belt and handed it to me.

The main obstacle—aside from the obvious one of going up the stick—was that I'd need something to replace the snapped stay. I hurried below, not that there was much hurrying to be done with the boat slamming around, and started digging through all the spare wire cable that was stowed underneath the cockpit, made up in fixed coils that hung on pegs. The great advantage of the *Mary Constance* was that it was a floating ship's store, filled with items that provide us with spares an ordinary vessel might not carry. I knew that one of the cable coils was a spare for the spring, and by comparing one with the other, I found the shortest one. That had to be it, and sure as rain, there was the label Mike had made me put on everything. I put a hook on one end and grabbed a turnbuckle for the other. The rest of the equipment I planned was a pretty simple rig, a luff tackle—a single block, a double block, and hooks at either end—but I knew it was going to be tough working at the mast tops. And when I say "tops," I mean both of them because the new stay would have to be fastened to each. Because Mike had used iron collars with eyebolts instead of rope grommets or lashings for the stay, the job looked to be pretty straightforward. Then it came to me that I didn't need the tackle, because with just a line attached to the cable I could pull it to the foremast when I got that far along in the job, and the scope in the turnbuckle should be enough to allow me to attach the cable and then take up the slack.

Having looped the coil of cable around my neck, the bulk of it hanging down my back so it wouldn't get snagged on anything on the way up, I went back on deck and prepared for the climb up. Although both Sam and Hump had demonstrated that they knew something about boat handling, neither seemed to know how to fashion a bowline on a bight, a knot that I could use as a bo'sun's chair. That took a few minutes to sort out primarily because of the way we were being thrashed about by the unforgiving waves. I didn't need the chair to climb up—I'd use the ratlines for that—but once I was there, I wanted to be able to use my hands as much as possible.

I tied a short line around my waist, leaving enough hanging on each end so that I'd be able to encircle the masts when I reached the tops. It's bad enough trying to hang on to the mast and do your work at the same time under the best of conditions, and these were damned close to the worst.

We fastened the bo'sun's chair to the end of the main halyard. I stuck my legs through the bights and buckled my belt around it to keep it from sliding down. I checked to see that I had my knife, my spike, and my pockets stuffed with marline and spunyarn. After telling them to pull the halyard just taut enough to keep the bo'sun's chair from slipping down around my knees, I started up.

I'm not great at geometry, but I can say truthfully that every so often the *Mary Constance* rolled at least thirty degrees to either side. That meant that the higher I went, the greater the arc would be as the masts swung from side to side. Not that the swinging is constant. When the hull is rolled down on one side, it sort of lies there for a moment and then slowly starts to move in the opposite direction, sometimes pausing along the way according to how the boat is being tormented by the waves. As I say, mathematics isn't my strong suit, but it didn't take a genius to recognize that thirty and thirty added up to sixty, and sixty degrees would be the arc that I'd be traveling when I got up to where the damage was. And there are occasions when the roll doesn't come slowly and you pick up speed as you're moving with the mast. What with the varnished wood doused like everything else with rain and spray, and the grease I'd smeared on so the gaff hoops would slide up and down easily, I'd have changed places with a monkey in an instant. We didn't have a monkey. We just had Sam and Percy-Hump—and me. And I was the animal sent aloft. Maybe I was a monkey, after all.

# { CHAPTER 26 }

It didn't take long to climb to the place where the stay was still attached to the iron collar around the main-mast. An eyebolt stuck out from the collar, pointing directly forward to the foremast collar, and it was through this eye that I'd have to secure one end of the new stay. First, I had to take off the end of the old stay, which was swinging out over the starboard side. The hook had been secured by a mousing of small line that was wound across its open part. It wasn't a time for saving string, so I got my knife out of its scabbard and sliced through the line. I couldn't risk dropping the old stay and its fitting down on deck. Sam and Hump would think I was trying to kill them, which might not have been a bad idea, but they'd probably return the favor when I got back down. I hated to do it, but I couldn't hang onto everything at once, so I just let the wind carry the old gear over the side. Then, I yelled down for Sam and Hump to haul hearty on the halyard and belay it. I didn't want to come barreling down so fast that I'd just leave a spot on the deck or else go rocketing off into the ocean if the line came loose.

Now, it may seem crazy to you—it does to me thinking about it—but I started laughing about then. I remembered Grandpa Mike's remark when he was told that some guy on a Nova Scotia long-liner had made a bet with some of his shipmates that he could hand-over-hand from the backstay up to the main top and then on over to the foremast and down to the deck. He did a pretty good job of it, making it all the way to the spring stay where one of his hands gave out and he went down to the top of the doghouse, cracking some wood and the bones in his legs. "He didn't understand the gravity of the situation," Mike said. I knew what gravity would do in my case.

Getting there, it turned out, had been the easy part. Now, I had to wrap one arm around the top of the mast to give myself some notion of stability, lock my legs around the mast, and with my free hand put the hook through the eye. Did you ever see an old woman whose eyes were pretty far gone try to thread a needle? She didn't have a thing on me. I poked the point of the hook at that damned eye over and over, but the way the Mary Constance was jumping around I kept missing the hole. Finally, I got it through the eye and just as quickly it popped right out. Hell and damnation! Again I tried, and this time, it went right through, and I was able to hold it with one hand and do an ugly but serviceable mousing with the other. My arms were shaking from the strain, and I wasn't even halfway through the job.

I couldn't let go of the other end of the cable because the swaying motion would set it swinging and either knock me silly or bust something else. Instead, I held the length of line I'd tied to the cable and, holding it tight, signaled for the pirates to ease off on the halyard so I could descend on the ratlines, still holding the bitter end of the line attached to the cable and letting it run through my fingers as I went down.

By the time I got to the deck, I was flat worn out. I knew I had to go back up on the foremast, but the way my muscles had been jumping up on the top of the main stick, I was afraid that they'd fail me on the second try.

"Shake 'em out," said Sam. "Shake your arms."

And he demonstrated by imitating old Bugle after a dunking. He took the end of the line to give me a chance to do the same. I did what he said, and my arms felt a little better. Time for the next trip up.

We knew that the old stay had come loose from the foremast because it had still been hooked on to the main. What we didn't know was whether the eyebolt on the foremast collar was still in good shape. From the deck, in the growing dark, it seemed that we could see that it was still there, but it was impossible to know if it had opened up and let the old stay loose, or whether the hook on the old stay had simply worked out, or whether the collar had parted. If the eyebolt was pulled open or the collar sprung, I'd have to jury-rig a rope collar at the top of the mast while being waved in the air like a flag.

Even if the eyebolt was perfect, the job was going to be a lot harder than before. It wouldn't do to simply take the new stay up and hook it on; it had to be pulled taut to take the strain off the masts. That meant I'd have to pull the cable close to the mast, secure the short line around it, shove the hook into the eyebolt on the collar, pull it until I had it tight as I could, and then twist the turnbuckle until the wire was as taut as a bowstring. It was a good thing that Grand-pa Mike had put cable wire on the *Mary Constance* because if I'd had to deal with something like the luff tackle I'd originally planned—two or three blocks, a big coil of rope, and all the rest of it—I might not have been able to get the job done. As it was, that little light piece of cable was getting heavy. Despite the line that secured it, it kept banging my legs as it whipped back and forth on the way up. How the hell was I supposed to hold on to the mast, pull on the cable, and then mouse it down so it didn't work loose? It was right on the edge of being impossible.

By the time I was five feet or so below the mast top, I could see that the eyebolt was whole and the old hook was still there, minus the cable that had been the stay. It had just snapped, I guess.

I climbed as high as I could on the ratlines but couldn't reach far enough around the mast to grab anything on the other side. It was as fat as the mainmast, and the shrouds that held the ratlines were slanted down at a sharper angle because this was a slightly narrower part of the boat, but for some reason—maybe it was just because I was bushed—I couldn't get around that damned stick. Another couple of years and my arms would have been longer. Right then, I wasn't sure I had another couple of years. I was forced to do what I didn't want to do. I untied the small line I had around my waist, and made sure those two characters down on deck understood that I wanted the halyard belayed and the bo'sun's chair secured. I watched as they did.

"Well," I said to myself. "Here goes nothing."

And I stepped into the air.

The two loops of the double bowline up around my thighs took my full weight and it felt as though they were going to cut my legs off. I needed those legs, too. They were now locked around the slippery foremast. I undid the short length of line tied around my waist, put one end as far around the mast as I could. Then, using the force of the wind to curl the other end around the mast, I grabbed it and made a quick knot. Now the line could take the strain as my body tick-tocked like a grandfather clock from one side of the mast to the other. At least I wouldn't be swinging out over the side if my legs gave way. But now I had another matter to deal with. My chest was so close to the mast that I couldn't get a free hand between so that I could pull the turnbuckle up to the eyebolt. I didn't want to untie the line holding me to the mast. I didn't want to, but I had to.

As soon as I untied the knot, I knew I had a fight on my hands. The bo'sun's chair held me up to the top of the mast, all right, but there was now nothing but my legs, hands, and arms to keep me from being thrown off to one side or the other. The wind was furious, the noise was insane, and I couldn't even tell what direction any of it was coming from. At that point, it came to me that I should have given this plan some more thought. Unfortunately, nobody was in a position to help me correct the situation, so I held on fast and worked my brain hard to come up with some way to hold onto the mast while still using my hands to pull on the line to tighten the new stay. The cable was now free, so I took a desperate swing, and after all my cold sweat and worry, pulled out the old hook, tossed it over the side, and clapped the cable hook into the eye on the first try.

The rest of it is a bit blurry. Maybe I was dizzy from being worked over up there, or maybe it was the fact that I was almost numb from cold. Wet, tired, and with that wind raking me constantly, I was shivering so much I wasn't sure I could do anything but let go. I know that I hauled hard on the line I had tied to the cable and must have put a dozen turns and half-hitches to mouse the hook, far more than I needed and just like a lubber, but I was so glad to finish the rotten job that I felt a blazing hatred for that stay. That bastard wasn't going to come loose again. The turnbuckle did what it was supposed to do as I twisted it with the point of my marlinspike, and I swear that I heard that stay change from a low note to a high one as I tightened it in the wind. Just before starting down, I took a deep breath and closed my eyes. When I opened them I saw again that faraway flash of the Highland Light, only this time it was off to port. We had been turned around.

ONCE I REGAINED THE DECK, I POINTED TO THE LIGHT, AND Sam and Hump stared as though it was at fault. It hadn't moved. We had. Without sails, we—they, to be accurate—had done a rotten job of keeping our heading, but I have to grant that they'd had to pay some attention to me while I was flailing about on high. With the spring stay now back in place, we could once again try to hoist something in order to heave to. First, we'd have to get some headway, and Sam and I undid the bo'sun's chair so we could reattach the halyard to the mainsail gaff.

Maybe he was at the helm, or maybe he was whistling "Away Rio" for all I know, but I couldn't tell you what that miserable Hump was doing while Sam and I wrestled and swore getting the halyard clapped onto the gaff. He had seemed to diminish all along the way, and where he had been fearsome and frightening at the outset, he now barely registered on my mind. All right. He did help some, but not a hell of a lot.

"Sam," I said, "as soon as we get the main up to the reef, I'm going below. I'm blowed."

He looked hard at me but just nodded. We both took a grip on the halyard and hauled handsomely until the gaff was up to the reef. Then, I did what I said, only before I could tumble down the ladder and lie on the cabin sole, Hump decided to chime in with a word or two.

"You clumsy sonofabitch," he sneered at me. "What took you all that time?"

Okay, I wasn't big, and I wasn't a grown up, but I'd had enough. They had never seemed to care that I had my marlinspike still shoved in my belt. I grabbed it by the lanyard on the top and pulled it out like a beardless Blackbeard with a cutlass, shoving the sharp point right in front of Hump's face. I screamed, "You scummy bastard! I'll fer you and I'll firk you and I'll ferret you!"

I still didn't know what it meant, but I figured if it was good enough for Shakespeare, it would do all right for me.

Hump drew back in terror, looking at me as though I was from a planet he'd never heard of. He wheezed out something that might have been an apology, but I really didn't care and fell below and collapsed. While the Mary Constance, the storm, and the pirates disappeared, I was somewhere that was soft and black and I never wanted to leave.

The two rogues up topside must have managed to wear the boat around because when I came to, it was once more to the easy rocking motion that meant we were once again hove to. I crawled over to the water breaker and drank right from the bung. Getting something besides salt in my mouth was a treat. I could have sat there for a long time, not really thinking about anything, just sort of hazy and unfocused, but down the hatch came Hump followed by Sam, and they appeared to be spent from whatever efforts they had been giving to get us comfortable again.

"This is damned foolishness," Hump offered to the cabin air as he sprawled again on the locker top.

"Right, you are," Sam agreed. "Tell me, Hump, just what other cute ideas do you have? We've got her riding easy again, we know pretty much where we are, and as far as I can tell, we're still afloat and looking to stay that way, so what's chafing your butt?"

"What's chafing my butt is that we were just going to snatch this tub and take a ride someplace and break it up, that's what. Instead, we're out here getting pounded like a bareknuckle pug, and we're no closer to bringing this thing to an end than we were last night."

Now I knew what they were up to. All along I had thought that they were going to take the *Mary Constance* to some port and maybe put a new name on her or try to sell her, but Hump let that old feline out of the sack.

"Where did you plan to take her?" I asked.

"Wellfleet or Sandwich or one of them places," Hump answered. "We could have run her up on the shore—hell, you couldn't keep her from running aground down there— we'd tear off the name, toss the papers overboard, and then we'd call in a salvor and cut a deal for maybe fifteen cents on the dollar and be on our way."

"You mean you'd intentionally wreck her?"

"Sure as fun," Hump responded. "We can sail a little, but we ain't in the saltwater trade. With a few greenbacks in the poke, we could cut out for someplace where we'd have an even start—maybe out west somewhere."

Sam hadn't said a word. He gazed at Hump with fixed eyes, and I couldn't tell whether he was angry or simply exhausted. Finally, he turned to me.

"It sounds hard, maybe. Hump's got a point. We need a fresh beginning, and these parts are filled up. Folks with money just get more, and those of us who don't have any don't have any way of catching up. And don't give me any guff about how every man has a chance in America. That's bullshit right down to the ground. Hump tells me he had worked hard before the mill shut down, and I believe him. I know I did where I was, and I was a floor supervisor. Do you think I was getting rich? Like hell, I was. And when the time came to shut down, so the owners could save money, I was pushed out the door with everybody else. Whatever pay I had in my pocket was all I was going to get, and the sonsofbitches took half of what was coming to me for what they said I owed them for things I'd had to buy to do my job. Sure, we're criminals now, but we weren't always, and with a fair shake and a new start, we'll do all right."

"But you can't just take my Grandpa's boat and wreck it for salvage!"

"Your grandpa, unless he's the idiot I don't think he is, has got insurance on this boat. It gets wrecked; he gets paid. Don't start whimpering about him. He's going to be a lot better off than we are."

"But she's a good boat. She's named after my mother."

"That's too bad, sonny. I wish it wasn't that way, but you'd better get used to the idea because as soon as we can, we're going to beach her."

That talk made me mad. I didn't care how tough things

had been for them, they had no right to break up a pretty boat like the *Mary Constance*. And, they could have asked Mike for money, and he'd have staked them if he thought they were worth it. I doubt if he'd have seen much worth in them, though. Even so, there were other things they could do. Hell, they could scavenge on the beaches, if everything else failed, and things were bound to get better sometime. There were some old men and women in Marblehead who probably hadn't seen a dollar in years, but they scrimped and helped out at their churches and got by one way or another. At the worst, there was always the Marblehead poor farm over on the Neck. But not these crooks. They'd rather take what somebody else had worked and saved for than to do the same thing themselves. They didn't look for other work when times were good, and when it went sour on them, they sat on their tails and howled. I ran right out of sympathy.

# CHAPTER 28

THE CABIN WAS FOGGED FROM A PIPE SAM HAD PULLED from somewhere in his clothes. I usually didn't mind it when Grandpa Mike fired up down in the cabin, but this stuff Sam was smoking smelled like tarred hemp, and I had stomach cramps from all that biscuit mush. I needed a breath of fresh air, so I pushed open the hatch and stuck my head out.

Bad move. The blast of air roared down into the cabin just as the boat heeled way over on her starboard side. The air was full of water, and I couldn't tell whether it was rain or spray, although it was probably both. I did taste more salt. Another blast hit us and this time we were pretty slow coming back up, besides which, we had been slammed down into a trough and had a fair chance of getting rolled unless things straightened out in a hurry.

But they didn't.

Ninety-nine times out of a hundred, a boat will stay on top of the water. Ninety-nine times out of a hundred, the natural floatation of the hollow wooden hull will keep her bobbing like a cork. One time out of a hundred, or maybe it's a thousand—I'm just guessing—all the rules are changed, and the combination of wind shoving the boat around to a direction it shouldn't be, and waves breaking against her side or over her decks until she is wallowing like a water-logged basket put the whole package in danger. That's where we were. I could see a wave curling up aft, rising higher and higher like a molten glass mountain, then it broke. The thing must have been twenty-five feet high and stretched out on either side for a couple of hundred yards. The top just leaned over too far and then fell right onto the stern of the *Mary Constance*.

I hadn't enough time to close the hatch door before water came pouring in like it was shot out of a fire hose. Charts, coffee pot, Sam and his pipe, Hump and his bonnet all went crashing toward the forward locker door. Stuff I didn't even know was on board shot through the air as if looking for new territory to settle in. Miraculously, the lamp, swinging in its gimbals, kept on burning, though it flickered wildly for a few seconds. Sam was flailing about, trying to get to his feet, and Hump was underneath him blubbering in the water that now washed to and fro atop the cabin sole. I closed the hatch.

"Jesus, save me!" Hump yelled.

"I'll save you, you awkward son of a bitch!" Sam answered.

"Get off my leg!"

"Get your damned foot out of my face!"

I was choking on sea water, which was a good thing, I guess, because if I had laughed the way I wanted to, those guys would probably have managed to swim back and kill me. Anyway, it wasn't that funny. Not until that jug of linseed oil made itself known.

I told you how I had secured everything in the forepeak locker, and I had. I did a good job, too, but when things go completely wild on a boat in a storm, there's really not much that stays put. The linseed oil stayed in the locker, but its cork apparently came out, because the water in the cabin quickly took on the sheen of oil globules coursing up and down. You know the old saying about how oil and water don't mix? Well, maybe not, but put them together and shake them up and you'll get the slickest mess you'd ever want to deal with. If pouring oil on stormy waves makes them calm, I'll allow that pouring linseed oil into bilge and cabin water did nothing to calm Sam and Hump.

Sam had just stood up, when his feet slipped up from under him and he landed on his butt, right on top of Hump, who had barely made it to his knees. They both went flat. Then, the two of them eeled around on the cabin sole, rising for a moment or two until they tried to take a step and then down they'd go. But they didn't stay put once they hit the deck because the boat would pitch or roll, and they'd slide from one end of the cabin to the other, clutching at the smooth sides of the storage lockers as they went by. The slick stuff got onto their hands and clothes and made things worse. They didn't even seem to be able to hold onto each other's hands.

I was still on the companionway ladder, with my feet out of the slop below, and saw no reason to join in the party.

"Gimme a hand," Hump bawled.

"Damn your hand!" was the sweet response from Sam.

Much as I hated to, I knew I'd have to get down there and start pumping again. The only way we'd ever get any order below would be when we could get the water down in the bilges again and wipe down the sole with whatever stuff we could find. I stepped straight down, not wanting to miss the ring in the bilge cover. I barely got there before I started to fall, but I caught myself on the mainmast, and lowered myself under control. With the cover off, I began to pump again, only this time I knew I'd never be able to do it all myself. I yelled to Sam to slip on up to where I was and hang onto the mast with me so we could take turns on the pump. He made it after a couple of tries, while Hump floundered up forward.

We pumped pretty fast, and, when he could, Hump came aft to join us. I scooted across the cabin to where a couple of canvas buckets were rolled up and brought them out. They worked pretty well as long as we made sure that their mouths were open when we dropped them in the water. Otherwise, they simply flattened out, and it was like pulling a rag across the deck instead of capturing the swill that was sloshing around. Working in a constant rotation, a few minutes on the pump and then back to the buckets, we dropped the water level in a fairly short time, but the planks of the cabin sole still resembled an ice-skating pond. Hump hauled himself up the base of the mast until he could open that dry goods locker with the scarves, linens, and finery, and we went to work wiping the deck as dry as we could. Mind you, all of this was going on while the boat bounced and tossed and threw us about.

Exhaustion finally got us. By then, with care and hand-holds, we were able to move around a bit, but we were so tired we just faked out on the locker tops and held on to keep from falling off.

We all slept. Or dozed, I guess, is more like it. You can't really relax when you feel like somebody has you by the shoulders and is shaking you until your teeth rattle. Also, the remnants of smoke from Sam's pipe, mingled with the reek of the oil that had recently sloshed over everything down below. Plus, the three of us were getting pretty gamy ourselves, and the cabin smelled high as a goat pen.

Maybe an hour had passed when things like smells lost all importance. Without warning, the *Mary Constance* heaved up and over on the starboard side. For a moment, it felt as if we were flying, and I suppose we were, because the hull lifted right up out of the water and then fell onto the water with a thump that seemed to signal the end of the world. But this time, we were over more than ninety degrees, and what had been the starboard side of the hull now became the floor. The overhead was now a bulkhead, and the cabin sole was the same. I was standing on the starboard side of the hull. I feared that we were going all the way over, turning turtle. If that happened, we might just head for the bottom.

I guess you can never know what a boat is going to do when it's upside down until you turn it that way and see what happens. Some have apparently floated that way for quite a while, trapping people inside. Mostly, they come back down, because the weight of the ballast and the keel are such that as the deck turns down to the water, they rise up and put things out of balance. Besides, most boats are not perfectly equal in the way weight is distributed. A locker on one side might hold a lot of heavy items, while one opposite might have lighter ones. Obviously, a good skipper would try to keep the weight pretty equal so that the vessel would keep an even keel, but there will always be differences. Some boats have rolled all the way 'round—doing 360 degrees—and usually losing most of their rigging in the process.

Down below, it was chaos, with everything breaking loose and zooming around the cabin. Things that were tied down and by all rights secured came hurtling through the air like bullets or bombs. Books from the captain's shelf jumped over their railings and wound up near the stove, which was not a particularly good thing since the door to the stove had popped open and dumped a pile of glowing coals into the cabin. Fortunately, the coals were brought up against the side of a locker and stayed pretty much in place. A fresh gush of seawater came cascading down the companionway ladder because the hatch had been carried away. That took care of the coals.

Then the Mary Constance came back down to where she was supposed to be, and we were upright once more.

But, Lord, what a mess! It was a complete jumble of just about everything Grandpa Mike had on board. Sure, he liked to keep things tidy, and he was a good seaman, but who could have planned on having a boat turn nearly upside down? And how would you ever be able to keep everything in place if you needed to use some of it, like a chart or a book or even the coffee pot? I don't know where that went. The water breaker was still where it had been, but it was tightly strapped onto its chocks, and they were screwed into the wood. It turned out that we didn't go all the way over, just far enough to put the main boom in the water and break it like a twig.

We didn't know that until we struggled up out of the cabin and saw the destruction caused by the knockdown: The jib boom was still in one piece, but it was swinging crazily across the foredeck, its lashings torn off, the sheet block slamming wildly from one end of the horse to the other; the main boom was broken from having dipped into the water and wrenched back up with a furled sail full of sea water; lines were loose and trailing over the side and astern; and the masts were quivering awfully.

No doubt we'd have to start pumping again before long, although I had little confidence that we'd be able to do much with all the sea drift of paper pulp, marline, chunks of coal, and God knows what sloshing around, any of which could and probably would stoak the pump and make our exertions futile.

And wouldn't you know it: that damned spring stay was parted again. This time, I wasn't going up to fix it.

THAT MUST HAVE BEEN THE WORST TIME. WE WERE ALL exhausted and unable to move quickly. From the way Sam and Hump looked, they were no more capable than I was of doing what needed to be done. We just hung on to whatever was handiest, staring into the darkness, ignorant now of where we were and barely able to tell which direction we were pointed. Finally, I crawled into the cockpit and looked at the compass. The binnacle lamp had been either blown out or had been drowned by the knockdown. There was only a slim chance that we'd be able to light a match in the wind that kept screaming, whipping spray in a never-ceasing sheet.

But, once more, the Highland Light. Now we saw it was abaft our starboard beam, and that meant we were headed down the Cape Cod coast. The wind had gone even farther to the northeast, apparently, because we were being driven downwind at a fairly swift pace. We had to maintain some kind of steering, if only enough to keep the waves from dashing aboard dead astern. Hump and I got the helm down, and it seemed to give us a little bit of offing from the coast. We needed more than that, I figured.

I lifted a coil of rope from a pin on the bulwark and tied a loop around my body just under my arms.

"Sam!" I yelled. "Hold this line and if I get washed over, pull me up!"

Now you may think it's a little odd that I'd ask a man who had threatened earlier to kill me if he'd pull me out of the water, but we three were no better than rats on a raft at this point, and if one of us could do something to help himself, he'd also be helping the others.

Neither Sam nor Hump asked what I was planning to do, and if they had asked I'm not sure that I'd have been able to tell them exactly. What did seem necessary was for us to raise some canvas so we could have some control over the direction the boat was taking. The main was too big, too wet, still lashed to the broken boom, and now unstayed at the top. I thought the jib had better possibilities, a smaller sail to put less strain on the foremast, even though that boom was still working like a scythe through the foredeck space. One whack from that piece of lumber, and I'd be Indian pudding.

I made that crawl once again over the cabin roof and then to the main mast where I rested and tried to make out what lay ahead. Surprisingly, there was some visibility because the white crests of the waves were easily seen up close, and it was against those that I spotted the jib boom, the furled sail still tied on, working like a mad horizontal pendulum, back and forth across the deck.

We should have tied a preventer of some sort on both

the booms when the wind first picked up, but no use crying about that now. Somehow, I had to settle the jib boom down so that I could let off the line that was holding the sail. I grasped at every line end that I could find by touch, pulling on each to see whether it was a jib sheet. Figuring that the bitter end might still be in the water, I slid down to the bulwark, ran my hand along the side of the hull and got a splinter. A hell of a way to start. Shortly, though, I encountered a stout line that was trailing alongside the boat. Ordinarily, you can tell immediately whether you have the correct line in your hands: You pull and something happens or doesn't. You know if it's right or not. This time, I was just lucky because the boom was swinging across the deck just as I hauled on the line and I managed to stop it as it made an unexpected pause amidships.

Fortunately, the jib halyard was still secured, and I heaved myself to my feet in order to release it and get some of the canvas up. God, but I was tired. Still, my muscles worked enough to get the jib up, and I belayed the halyard with a satisfied groan. I grabbed the now useless peak halyard from the foremast, figuring I might use it to brace it up a little. Then, once more, I scratched my way down the deck to the cockpit and another collapse on the grate. I handed the halyard end to Sam and told him to tie it off. Obviously, it wasn't as good as a stay for the foremast, but used as a makeshift backstay it might help keep it up. Now, at least, we should have some control over the boat.

Sam took over the helm, and we were soon running before the wildest waves we had seen, great rows of charging white that broke in ranks behind us. The warp we had streamed behind us now took a tremendous strain, doing the job for which it was intended, that is, to slow us enough that we didn't surf over one crest too fast and bury our bow in the wall of the next one. That would have been instant disaster because going at speed, if we plowed bow down into the back of a high wave, the boat would have been pitch-poled, tossed ass over teakettle, and not many survive such a calamity.

I decided that I had to try to get that binnacle lamp going again, or we'd just be feeling our way in the dark with only an occasional light on shore to give a clue as to our location. But that wasn't the main reason: we had to have the compass so that we could steer with the waves. That may sound silly, but we really couldn't see them too well. The scend of the following sea raised the stern out of the water from time to time, and the rudder, unable to bite into anything but air, was useless at those moments. That posed the danger of us coming down sideways, and then we'd stand a very good chance of cashing in everything.

I removed the lamp from the binnacle and told Sam that I'd need a hand when I came back topside.

It took three trips. On the first two forays, the lamp blew out as soon as I got back on deck. On the third try, I managed—with Sam's help—to get my slicker over the binnacle cover and then lift that and slide the lamp in between gusts. We were once more able to point in a known direction. Not that we could do anything about going in a different one. At least it made us feel better and it did improve the ability to keep the onrushing waves on our tail.

Now, we had two major worries, not that the little worries

were over: we needed the jib to allow enough steerageway to keep from running into the shore, and we needed that foremast to stay up. If the foremast went down from the strain of the wind coming from aft, then we'd have no jib, and no real chance of keeping offshore. If the jib blew out, we'd be back under bare poles, able to scud before the wind in some manner but unable to claw off the Cape. Either way, there was not much more that we could do.

The Highland light was intermittent, perhaps because of low clouds and rain, or perhaps we had begun to outrun its range. But there were other lights, according to the chart, and if they were still working in this blow, they should give an idea of how far and how fast we were traveling. All I could think of was that chart I had seen on the table showing the long bar that ran due south from Chatham and the seeming wall of shoals at its tip, pierced only by a little opening right near Chatham and after that, if we were foolhardy enough, that channel through Pollock Rip, both as good as unmarked in the darkness and the storm.

We barreled along like blind men in a whirlwind with no idea of when this lunatic ride was going to end. If it was possible, the storm had become stronger and, for sure, the waves that came roaring up behind us were taller, surging up in a liquid threat that was so fearsome that I didn't even want to look aft.

Hump saw it first. "There's another light," he sang out, and Sam and I both lunged toward starboard to get a sight of it. Only it wasn't one light; it was three, dim little things just off the bow. That had to be the Three Sisters Lighthouses a little north of Chatham, and we were well north of them.

Lord, we must really be rolling along! From one end of the Hook down to Chatham must be close on forty miles, and we appeared to be about halfway down the coast.

I was almost enjoying it, except that at the back of my mind were all those worrying questions that wouldn't keep quiet: Where were we aiming to put in? Even with the compass, how were we going to navigate those close quarters? If we were going into Chatham, we had to make a run past the town and down to a narrow spot between Chatham Harbor and Monomoy Island, and how the hell could we do that in the dark? Oh, we could make the turn all right, risking a broach in the process. However, we wouldn't have even a vague idea of where we were doing it.

Had Sam and Hump realized that they were now just trying to save their own necks and had given up any idea of getting rich from their thievery? Were they going to keep me on board as we tried for a safe haven, or were they going to ship me over so I couldn't tell anybody what they had done? And the biggest question: was the *Mary Constance* going to wreck herself and drown us all so that nobody would ever know what happened?

# { CHAPTER }
# { 30 }

THE "THREE SISTERS" STAND OFF TOWARD THE COAST FROM Eastham, a small village up on higher ground. The idea of putting up three lighthouses, instead of just one, was so that people at sea, as we were, would be able to distinguish them from anything else and get a sense of location during the night. They were low, squat structures, and their lights were weak, but they were doing their job as far as we were concerned. I'd heard about the three lighthouses all the way up in Marblehead because a lot of folks were critical of the plan, saying it was a waste of money and that anybody who was on the water should be able to tell one light from another. They were willing to grant that maybe two lights might be helpful, as they are up on Thachers Island, but that three were just excessive. That fellow named Thoreau even wrote about the Three Sisters, and he was pretty harsh, but he wrote something else that I liked. I wish I could remember it exactly. It was something to do with the fact that you don't have to stick all your life in one place, that the stars twinkle in other places, too. That's what I believe, too, but not many adults give that kind of advice. Unfortunately, I couldn't see any stars in any places where we were, but you get the idea.

Actually, that there were any lighthouses at all down along this stretch of the Cape was something of a miracle. Nobody knows how many boats and ships have been wrecked along this shore or how many sailors have died here. Timbers and planks don't last long here because the locals carry them off as soon as they can, and not so long ago the people made much of their living from picking apart the hapless hulks that smashed up on their beaches. In fact, there were people in Chatham who fought like hell to keep a lighthouse from going up there because it would give the sailors too good a chance to avoid disaster. These bastards shook their fists and swore at full moons, lights they couldn't control, which offered vessels in distress a visual sighting of the shoreline dangers.

Suddenly, we heard a great "Crack!" from somewhere forward, and my heart almost stopped. I thought the foremast had broken off. No, it was still up, but that noise couldn't mean anything good was happening up there. It could have fractured someplace and still been able to stay up—for a little while. With no way to maintain steerageway, except in a most elementary sense, we had to have the jib flying.

Sam, hard at the helm, looked dazed and exhausted. Hump was huddled down against the cockpit coaming, his head lowered so that I couldn't have seen his face even if there had there been enough light. Of course, he still had that damned dumb bonnet on so that would have hidden him even more. We were all soaked and wretched from the rain, the spray, the pounding of the boat, and the drain on our nerves and muscles. A fresh crew might have been able to come up with some better ideas on what to do, but we were down to the dregs of our energy, and I, at least, was just beginning to believe that we were doomed. I imagine the other two felt the same, and Hump might already have crossed the line. Some people may not understand what I'm saying, that somebody as young as I would be willing to give the slightest consideration to giving up. That's because they've never been put through what we had for the past—my God!—was it only twenty-four hours?

The *Mary Constance* moved on, the wind now raging over the port quarter, pushing us closer to the shore, although we were still some distance off. Every time Sam tried to make a point further offshore, a wave would thump us back to the original course, and the whole thing began to take on an inevitable cast, something so much bigger than we or the boat could deal with.

I thought of Grandma Ellen and Grandpa Mike and the house we lived in, brown shingles, gabled roof, the little garden in the back, and the flowers Grandma tended so carefully every summer day. I was almost sure that I could see them there, and then I seemed to wake up, realizing that I was not likely to see them again. It occurred to me, in that half dream, that Grandpa Mike must be back from Boston, in fact probably had been for most of the afternoon, and that he'd be sending telegrams all around the Bay and the Cape asking for information about the *Mary Constance* and me. Not that it would do any good right now with the only possible help coming from on shore and the shore now our greatest fear.

And I thought about Ez and Bugle—and how Ez just wouldn't believe that I'd been lost in a storm. He and I were friends, and I didn't have any others who were as much fun. I wondered if Bugle would miss me. He wasn't my dog, even though I spent almost as much time with him as Ez did, but you can't be sure what a dog might feel. He'd probably get over it. All you'd have to do is get him a stick.

And what about Agatha? Would she miss me? And for how long? Would she grow up and marry some snob from Boston or Cambridge and never have a thought about me? Or would she live on for years as a spinster, pining for her friend from schooldays? Why would it matter to me, anyway? I wouldn't know about any of it. Still, I'd hate to think of Agatha married to somebody from Boston, or—God save us!—New York!

Well, I was damned if I was going to let my feelings slide down any lower. All the people and the one dog I cared about were on shore, I was on the ocean, and the two things were totally disconnected. Later, if we made it through this sail-ripping sonofabitch of a storm, I'd take the time to tally up who and what was important to me. Right now, I was the only thing that mattered—along with Sam, of course, and that cringing Hump who was important only if he could be of some help.

"He's a Jonah!" Hump had roused from his depression and was glaring at me with all the hate he had been holding in.

"Belay that!" Sam roared in reply.

"No! He's a Jonah, and he'll kill us both! Ever since we found him on board, things have been going to hell. If we don't put him over the side, we'll be wrecked and drowned!"

"I said to stow it," said Sam. "Things were going to hell for us long before we got on this boat, and he's done his share to keep us afloat."

"He's going to get us killed!" Hump persisted.

"If you don't shut up, we'll see who gets killed. I said to stow it."

Hump wasn't mollified, but he didn't say anything else. He didn't have to because he kept staring holes through me from under the brim of that idiotic headgear which was now sodden and nearly shapeless, and I found it more comfortable to move as far away from him in the cockpit as I could. I could possibly kill him with marlinspike or knife, but, Jesus! I'm not a killer!

I took a firm grip on a chock that was nailed to the deck, figuring that if he made a jump for me, he'd have to be lucky to pull me loose before Sam got to him. I was assuming, of course, that Sam would stop him, although the more I thought about it, the less sure I was that I could count on his help. After all, he was the first one who had threatened me, even though he now seemed to be taking up for me. It didn't seem to make a lot of difference when I considered the mess we were in. There was little chance that any of us would make it through the night.

On we rocketed along the coast, a coast that got closer, inch-by-inch. Or maybe it was foot by foot—how could we tell? All that was for sure was that we couldn't claw away from the coastline. The waves were so strong that coming about was out of the question, and the strain on the rig in any such maneuver was bound to be disastrous. As long as we had that handkerchief of a jib flying, we still could hope that the wind would back enough to give us a bit of offing. So far, however, it came right over the port quarter, pushing, always pushing us bit by bit toward the uncaring coast of the Cape and always trying to break the foremast in two.

Then, what we had feared.

# CHAPTER
## 31

IT WAS LIKE A RIFLE SHOT. THE FOREMAST WENT. THE SHARP
report of the big spruce spar snapping about four feet off
the deck made us all jump up and grab something for support. The mainmast, because the spring stay had parted, was
safe for the moment, no longer being attached to the broken spar. But that foremast was terrible trouble. Its starboard
shrouds were still attached to the fallen, shattered mast, now
hanging in the water, banging against the boat. It seemed
that the port cables hadn't parted, although we couldn't
be sure at first. Now, I began to question whether Grandpa Mike had been so smart, after all, when he replaced the
old rope shrouds with metal. With rope, you simply sawed
away with a sharp knife, but cable was a different bag of eels,
and those fancy turnbuckles were bent and stretched, the
chainplates holding them still intact but deformed. Whatever we were going to do, we had to get started immediately,
or that long hunk of wood was going to knock the planks
right off us. Also, the drag in the water of the fallen spar and
canvas would act to point us more toward the shore, and

we were in enough trouble on that count as it was.

I looked at Sam. Sam looked at me. Neither of us looked at Hump, which kind of tells you where things had dropped to at that point. I didn't even consider that Hump was going to contribute anything in the way of a solution to our problem, and Sam wasn't giving off any sparks of brilliance either. I remembered that Mike kept a couple of axes on board, for when he used driftwood instead of coal, as he sometimes did. They were stowed under a stern hatch, which was marked by a ringbolt that served as a handle to open it with. When I popped it open, I expected to be able to reach down and grab an axe handle, but the way the Mary Constance had been whirling and twirling in the water for the past few hours everything had married with everything else and it took a bit of rustling about in the dark to finally get both of the tools.

I passed one blade out to Sam and took the other for myself. Together, we made our way forward, cautiously, I needn't tell you, because every time the boat rolled or pitched I was afraid I'd have my legs sliced off by a whipping shroud, while the broken foremast leaped and thundered against the side of the boat. By the time we got far enough forward to figure out where things were, we could see that the port shrouds were holding—in fact, they were the only thing taking any strain. When the mast snapped, the force of the wind had shoved the sail, the boom, and all the lines over the starboard side.

The forestay was slack, and the starboard shrouds were merely sawing at the rail. The port shrouds had kept the whole mess from breaking free and were taut across the deck hooked on the big bitt on the foredeck, which kept them from sliding aft to the stump of the broken mast. That bitt, a square strong block of oak with a half-inch iron plate on top, would be a big help if we were able to horse the shrouds on top of it and—and this was a lot scarier—if we were able to direct the blow of an axe onto the cable without taking off the hand or head of the other guy.

Before we did anything else we had to clear the forestay from the bow, a job that was surprisingly easy because the stay was under no strain and wouldn't be until we freed the port shrouds from the deck. The same was true of the starboard shrouds: the turnbuckles worked the way they were supposed to, and the shackles holding them to the chainplates gave up without a fight.

I guess sometimes I'm not quite bright, because I grabbed at a shroud, tried to pull it, and found it didn't budge, and probably never would. But Sam managed to get the end of his axe handle under one of the shrouds, the lower one, I think, and levered it up onto the metal plate. That meant we'd have to swing away hoping that a lucky hit might bite into the cable. Sam and I looked at each other, sort of shrugged, and began to chop. It was then I saw that he was having enough trouble just keeping his feet and that any hope for accuracy in his stroke was going to be pretty slim. He didn't seem to worry that I was in his range, and he brought the blade whistling across, sending sparks jumping, but he severed one of the cables with the blow. The next one wasn't as easy, the edge of the axe blade bouncing off at a crazy angle and nearly catching me in the face.

"Shit, Sam!" I cried. "Be a little more careful!"

"Sorry, Sonny. I'm being as careful as I can."

He fired a couple of more ricochets and finally parted the other shroud. We both believed that the foremast alongside the boat would immediately fall away, but there was a gnarl of lines that groaned and held, and, naturally with our luck, the starboard shrouds were tangled on something and were now holding firm.

I grabbed the second axe and just started slashing away at the rat's nest of lines with nothing but good solid wood underneath it. It would have been better had I been able to get an angle that would have allowed me to chop down against the chainplate or something just as hard, but that wasn't in it. I was mad as hell, probably a lunatic at that point. The damned blade kept bouncing off until I thought it would never give up, but it finally did and we watched the spar with its train of mangled lines, ripped sail, and nearly all of our remaining hopes float free behind us.

Well, I don't need to tell you again that we weren't going to do much sailing then, but that didn't mean we were completely done for. The boat was scudding along and wallowing, sure enough, but the rudder still gave a little control—not much, but a little.

The idea of a rudder is that the water running past it puts pressure on one side or the other, depending on which side the rudder is positioned. At the moment, it seemed that the wind was driving us just a mite faster than the water we were riding on, although it was traveling in the same direction. We generally managed to keep the bow in line with the motion of the waves, at least enough to keep us stern-to-the-wind. If we wandered too much, the boat would broach, and that might finish us.

At that point, Hump quit. He just gave up. Sam yelled at him and threatened him, and it had no effect whatsoever. Sam called him a chicken-livered, good-for-nothing sonofabitch and a couple of other things I'd never heard before but which I'm pretty sure were not compliments. It made no difference. Hump had collapsed onto the cockpit floor and sat there, all doubled up, wailing that he was going to be drowned, and why did this have to happen to him, and that he was a good man who was trying to do right, and all kinds of other claptrap that apparently was addressed toward Providence. He sure wasn't going to get any sympathy from the remaining crew of the *Mary Constance*.

I think we all began to hallucinate about then. I know I did. I thought I saw Bugle standing on shore just as if he were real. And the damnedest thing is that he had his chin pointed up in the air and he was baying! Like a champion. I tried to tell it to the other two, but they paid no attention. Shortly afterward, Sam yelled that he could see a big steamer dead ahead and that we were going to ram into her, but we really couldn't see anything in the dark. We all strained to see, and even Sam admitted that if he had seen it, he couldn't any longer. As for Hump, hell, I think all he was doing was moaning and carrying on about everything from his sins to his love for his dear old mother. We were edging always closer to the Cape's elbow, and, if we tried to get into Chatham, we'd have to make a decision pretty soon. I wasn't confident that we'd be able to control the boat once we tried to turn her or even whether we could get any response from the rudder if we put it over. My earlier belief that we could maneuver had pretty much been washed and blown away, leaving me with a cold feeling in my stomach and nothing that I could call hope anywhere in my body.

When people say storms are fickle, they know what they're talking about. All of a sudden, the wind began to abate, not entirely, of course, but it was clearly not as strong. Then it died some more and then more. It was as though it was as tired of the whole thing as we were. But there was no relief from the waves. They kept pummeling us, and now we had no steerage at all—or damned little. The *Mary Constance* was tossed like sea scum, up and across, down and back. Violent moves. We were going to be beaten to death before we were finally cast into the murky madness of the water.

This went on for some time—fifteen minutes, maybe. We all lay on the deck, grimly holding onto anything that offered a solid handhold. We were shaken so much that I began to hurt inside, like my guts were being separated from each other, my liver heading for where my kidneys used to be, and my lungs probably trading places with my intestines.

And then it got really bad.

{ CHAPTER }
# 32

HOW THESE THINGS WORK, I JUST DON'T UNDERSTAND. FOR hours and hours the wind had backed around in a counter-clockwise fashion, first out of the northwest, then west, then southwest, south, east, and so on, until the fiercest part of the blow came from the northeast. It was supposed to keep on moving away from us and finally allow for some respite. Now, the lull had ended and the damned wind was coming at us, nearly as strong as before, and from the southeast again!

Southeast! A building breeze ramming into a wave train out of the northern quarter setting up mountains of saltwa-ter, waves that rose monstrously and then, as if unable to bear the weight, collapsed from the top in thundering cascades. We were unable to do a thing but hold on, and even then the wash of the sea over our bodies nearly swept us away.

The boat weathercocked toward the wind, her bow leap-ing and plunging, then swung wildly off to starboard as the wind caught her and the still-seething southwestward tend-ing waves pushed against her flanks. Now, there was no lon-ger a question about when we were going to put in to shore—

the wind had decided that for us. The "where" was still to come, and we had nothing to say about it.

Hopelessly and helplessly we drove on through the murk and madness of the night. Hump was prostrate, not even moaning any longer, save for an occasional plea for Jesus to deliver him. I wished he'd deliver him to someplace else. Sam had lowered his head onto his chest, where his beard stuck out in a salt-rimed fringe. I tried desperately to think of something, anything, that I could do or that Sam and I might do together that would give us a chance of saving the ship, but only visions of drowning in a cold, merciless sea appeared. I tried to think of things onboard that would float, that might hold us out of the water. Again nothing. Well, for a moment, I did consider emptying the water breaker and trying to hold onto it if I were cast into the sea, but the thought of going below, wresting the damned thing loose from the chocks that held it, and then hoisting it up the ladder on my shoulder while the ship was breaking up seemed senseless.

Waves smacked us from all directions, it seemed, yet the *Mary Constance* was driven forward to some unseen destination, crewless, for all that we could do to guide her. From somewhere in the roar of the ocean, a new sound came to me, a dull crashing, muffled and terrifying. Somewhere out there ahead of us was a shoreline, and I was hearing the storm-savaged surf smashing against it. It wouldn't be long before we were part of it.

Sam yelled something—I couldn't make it out clearly, but I heard the words "We'll make it." I don't know whether what went before was "I don't think…" or "there's no chance that…" or maybe even "I hope…." Whatever it was, it sure as hell wasn't going to affect what was going to happen. We were in the hand of the sea, and it was going to toss us or guide us wherever it wished. We were on a derelict. So much for seamanship and knowing how to sail. From here on, it was dumb luck, good or bad, and hugging wet planks and spitting out salt water.

I suppose you know about beaches, how they shimmer in bright sunshine and how you can sift the sand between your toes and jump around and fall down on the yellow cushion it provides. But have you ever walked along the very edge of the water where the grains of sand are packed together like concrete? Have you ever stamped the heel of your foot down on that stuff and found that you barely left an impression? Well, that's what we were heading for unless something changed in a hurry—a low, shelving wall that lurked under the surface and waited for us to challenge it. And you can add in the fact that boulders hide in those sands.

The surf sound grew louder, now distinctly audible as the waves piled against the shore, roaring, churning, with a cadence out of hell. Even Hump—poor old Percy, the bastard—stopped lamenting and begging for divine assistance, and Sam seemed dazed and drained. He raised his head from his chest and stared fixedly ahead, not seeing anything that I couldn't see, but seeming to be almost mesmerized by something out there just beyond his focus. I tried to make out the surf line, but the darkness hid the land and what lay between us and it. The shallower it got, the steeper the waves became as they rolled up from the deep ocean bottom and met the resistance of the sand.

Then, as though a curtain lifted, I saw an awful boil of

white, a pulsing shatter of acres of water as it broke against what was still unseen. A hundred yards? Fifty? I couldn't tell. All I knew is that we were hurtling toward it, out of control.

Each big wave that came up from behind lifted the stern high enough that I could now make out individual trains that were smashing against the shore. Closer and closer— would we scrape the bottom first, then be lifted onto the beach? That was the one hope I still held. But that was dashed like the waves.

We hit full on, as though a giant hammer had been swung into the bow. The three of us at the steering well were slammed against the after bulkhead of the cabin top. I heard the thunderclap of the breaking mainmast as it was hurled forward and then crashed onto the deck. Again and again, the waves pounded the *Mary Constance* with brutal force against the hard-packed sand, and terrible wrenching sounds carried up to me as planks were sprung and wood splintered.

From that point on, I really can't tell you what happened. I was in the water, trying to swim, but pummeled and pushed so strongly that my arms and legs seemed useless against the forces that held me. Each time I managed to lift my face out of the water, I was shoved back down so rapidly that I scarcely snatched a breath before being submerged again. The water was like a slurry of sand, muck, water, tiny fragments of sea shells, and who knows what. Finally, I ceased fighting. Nothing, nothing I did made any difference. What strength I had earlier was now gone and so, I decided, was I.

The last thing I remember was being thrown through the air and then a wrack of pain as I landed on something.

"I THOUGHT HE MOVED."

A voice, a woman's voice. I didn't recognize it, and I wanted to see who it was, but my eyes wouldn't open.

"See, his eyelids are fluttering." The same voice, and I still couldn't see where it came from.

"Well, let's see if we can get some hot tea into him. Gotta warm him up somehow." This time, the voice was a man's, deep and strong.

I heard clattering, kitchen noises, and then a hand was placed beneath my head and lifted me. At last, I opened my eyes, which didn't see too well, just a blur of faces, which soon came into focus. Five or six faces hovering over me and not a one belonging to anybody I had ever seen before. They all began to smile. A woman in a blue apron put her hand on my forehead and stroked it.

"Good gracious, boy," she said. "We thought you were gone for certain."

"I hope I'm not," was all I could come up with.

They all began to chatter at once, each one saying something about how I needed some color in my cheeks, or did I have enough covers on me, or how did I get there, or what was my name. It all ran together and confused me until that first man's voice boomed out,

"Give him a drink of tea. Poor kid can't answer anything until he's cleared his head."

Until that minute, I can say that nothing in my life ever tasted as good as that hot, sweet cup of tea that the man held for me to drink. It may even have been too hot, but the way I felt no scorched tongue was going to stop me from draining the cup as fast as I could. I felt it splash down to my insides and immediately began to warm me up. It was perfect. And I don't even like tea.

We eventually got around to sorting out some of what had happened. I was asking as many questions as they were. They wanted to know who I was and where I was from, and I wanted to know what happened to the *Mary Constance* and any men who had been on board with me.

At that, the man—his name was Caleb Morris—pulled a long face and said that he hoped if there were any that they weren't my kin. I almost blurted out that I was damned if they were any kin of mine, but I figured that what with the women there and all I'd better mind my language. I was tempted to say that they were a couple of rogues and crooks, but I held my tongue on that also.

"No, sir. They were no kin. I just happened to meet up with them. The two of them."

"Well, the Lord took 'em both, I guess. We found one fellow, well, I don't know how to describe him except that he was wearing some sort of a fool bonnet on his head. Didn't have any hair under it. He was rolled up like a ball in a mess of rope that was tangled around him. No sign of the other one. Who were they?"

"I really don't know," I replied. Somehow, it seemed better to just let them go. From what I'd learned, they didn't have much in the way of families, except Hump claimed to have a mother. She might not have been willing to claim him.

I wish I'd known Sam under different circumstances. He might have been someone who could have been, if not a friend, then at least a decent sort of fellow. He might have got a job at the sawmill or on the railroad, or when times got a little better he might have wound up working at Bassett's shoe factory. If you put him up against a guy like that sneaky Sanders, I think I'd have gone with Sam. He had shown that he was able to change his attitude toward me as we fought the sea side by side, and he was willing to take on that crazy Hump to see that I had the same chances the two of them had as the end approached. Maybe I should have hated him for what he did to the *Mary Constance* and Grandpa, but it wasn't in me at the time.

But they didn't find any sign of him, which was odd.

As for Hump, well, let him go. He was nothing but one big complaint. Maybe people should stop talking about having a Jonah on board and start worrying whether they've got a Percy.

I told the Morrises who I was and who my grandparents were, and one of the men hustled off to send a telegram to Marblehead. About an hour later, we got a reply from Mike and Grandma Ellen saying they were on their way down to

Chatham by the earliest means and they were happy that I was all right. It took them most of the day to get there, and all the people in Chatham gathered to greet them and bring them over to the Morris' house where we hugged each other and Grandma Ellen cried and Grandpa Mike said that he couldn't afford to hire a boy to replace me so I'd better get up and about as soon as I could. And maybe I could get a dog.

Another family put them up for the night, and I stayed with Mr. and Mrs. Morris, getting treatment a king would envy, with cod cakes and dumplings for dinner and a chunk of apple pie that would hold me close to the ground in a strong wind. They were really nice folks, considering that I was a total stranger with a sketchy story who had literally washed ashore on them. I couldn't imagine that they would have had neighbors who would cuss at the moon.

In the morning, Grandpa Mike and I walked down to the beach and saw the wreck, the little that was left of it. There wasn't much of the pretty little boat. Some of the frames had dug into the sand and stuck up like the inside architecture of a whale, and the waves, now a lot less angry but still powerful, coiled spume around them. The beach was littered with boards and broken objects of all kinds, tatters of sail and snarls of line, including the rode we had used as a drogue. It was tangled into a rat's nest and hooked onto what used to be the rudder. Apparently, the bottom had split on the sand and spilled just about all of Mike's inventory into the water. It wasn't very deep, so there was hope that some of it could be salvaged, although I could tell from Mike's eyes that his heart wasn't concerned with the business of recovering bits of brass, wood, and iron.

He walked up to one of the skeletal frames and put his hand on it.

"She was a nice boat, Luke. She was a nice boat."

I just swallowed hard.

"I guess we better get started back," Grandpa said and turned his back on the remains.

"Just a while, Grandpa."

I walked northward along the beach, examining the dunes where pieces of the vessel had been thrown by the storm and its remnants. I figured that if I looked long enough and hard enough I might find it, and finally I did. Torn away whole and undamaged, bright as new except for some streaks of dried salt, gleaming in the morning sun, and heavier than I had expected, it could have weighed a ton and I'd still have carried it. Grandpa saw me coming with it, wiped at his eyes with one hand, and then gave me a big smile.

"We'll need this for the new one," I said proudly, showing him the board that bore the gilded name: *Mary Constance*.

"Good boy, Luke. We've got work to do in Marblehead."

## { EPILOGUE }

I DON'T REALLY HAVE ANYTHING TO ADD TO THE STORY, but I wanted to have an Epilogue. It sounds pretty fancy.

There's one thing: it was terrible that we lost the boat, but at least I never had to tell Grandpa Mike that I peed in his turpentine.